The Words You Were Looking For

An Anthology of
Winners and Finalists
from the 2025
San Francisco Writers Foundation
Writing Contests

First Edition

Designed and Produced by Lissa Provost and
Edited by E Provost at
New Alexandria Creative Group
For the San Francisco Writers Foundation

NewAlexandriaCG.com
SFWriters.org
Available everywhere via print on demand.
Please support your local bookstores.
Print ISBN: 978-1-64715-013-6
eBook ISBN: 978-1-64715-014-3

Dear Reader,

For the first time in my tenure as a director of the San Francisco Writers Conference, the Grand Prize Winner of our annual writing contest comes from the poetry category. Our judges pick the finalists and category winners, and the conference planning team and board vote for the Grand Prize from among them. It's always a difficult decision, but the poetry winner this year demanded our votes. ***Waltz at Dusk*** makes the mundane magical. We now understand the beauty of raising goats.

As I began to edit this anthology, looking for a theme to emerge, I found a wealth of magnificent imagery among the finalists. From this, our theme became this volume's title. In ***The Words You Were Looking For***, you'll find an invitation to see the world like our winning poet in the first entry of a nonfiction mindfulness guide, ***Indra's Net***. You'll visit an old family homestead through the eyes of a child in ***The Pearl Farmers***. You'll bloom with ***Self-Portrait as Frida Khalo's Flower of Life On My First Motherless Mother's Day***. Then maybe contemplate revenge on a quietly terrifying other world in ***The Water Bank***.

In addition to these amazing category winners and all the fantastic finalists, this volume contains the five winning entries of our first Microfiction contest! After many years of seeing "please add flash fiction" on feedback forms, we're excited to be able to add this contest and a Flash Fiction track to the 2026 writers conference. The contest was held on our Discord server, where our community connects throughout the year.

While social and traditional media bombards us with escalating intensity year after year, these writers have stepped away from the noise to see what is lovely about the world. And they've crafted words that can take us with them. Those are always the kind of words we're looking for.

CONGRATULATIONS! To all our finalists and winners. We look forward to more beautifully crafted words from you as you bloom in your careers.

Sincerely,

Lissa Provost and The San Francisco Writers Conference Executive Board

Find out more about the San Francisco Writers Conference and Foundation, including our next contest, at SFWriters.org.

Contents

The Words You Were Looking For
Poetry

Adult Nonfiction

Adult Fiction

Children's and YA

Microfiction

POETRY

Grand Prize Winner:
Waltz at Dusk
by Emily King

Everything is living here,
stones breathe between pink toes and foam froths at my heels.
They beg to sweep me away,
to ignore the layer of disregarded chocolate foil and grocery bags
and dive where mollusks hide under their mantle capes,
purring lullabies through their fleshy gills.

I bury my palms underneath the wet,
arms warm and hands cool,
cold, full of grit
that tastes of salted dirt.

———————————

Somewhere,
a Kea cracks his beak into a snail
splintering her parts-
an eggshell.
Her body runs like yolk across the dry ground.

The bird nuzzles its olive head
into old wings-
Each bone sliding tender
along the soft of his skull.

———————————

Thousands of them- or at least two dozen-
stomp their toes across a lush field.
They stare at me,
coarse hairs moving in the wind.

Rectangle pupils pulse in the heat
and nod in a swimming motion-
around and over, around and over
watching flies crawl across their eyes
pressing one sticky foot i n f r o n t o f t h e o t h e r-
tangling into the wool on their backs
and under their bellies.

I can feel the oil on each strand of white
rubbing between my thumb and first finger.
It seems it is time for shearing.

Heaviness-
the bulk of his body presses into my shins,
legs prostrate.
This sheep has done this a summer ago
but I am not sure if he collects memories
the way we do-
shelved in glass jars waiting to be opened.

I wonder what I have not collected.

———————————————

Our seasons are hours-
Felt in night's hibernation
And the spring of morning
Dew crusts between the lashes on my eyes
and microscopic hairs that span me slowly regrow
with the day.

The moon reflects the sun
the same way that I reflect the countryside-
barely,
my skin a shadow of the landscape
my hair the reds of the reeds.

———————————————

I peel back a fingernail
And bury it under roots,
Imaging that parts of me will grow
into the DNA of a Eucalyptus.

How tall will these trees be
when earthworms come to kiss
the places that have gone untouched,
the sockets of my eyes and the soft pink of my throat?

———————————————

The Queen of these woods
has a map of the Subterranean
etched into her palm.

She has referenced it only once
when Fairyflies slept in those warm spaces.

Her plinth is plump with sap
and sugar
that surges and pools
at the rings of her wrists.

―――――――――――――

The mountains are calling
and I must listen-
let my feet sink into the sweat at their base
and worship at their feet.

Mother,
Transcribe the hill's vibrato
the summit's song-
compose a waltz
to feed to the Bellbirds of the winter.

When my boots have dismantled themselves-
when my hips and elbows and shoulder blades
have felt the pulp of the snow-
I can pitch myself forward and look below
I can imagine how minuscule
I must seem to the peaks.

―――――――――――――

Darkness sucks at my teeth
pushing between my ears
and under my hair.
My freckles are marks of nightfall
and in the blackness
everything seems to float-

Sheep curl on top of one another
suspended in time.
Deer fold and shift in ink
unaware that their antlers
are piercing holes in the atmosphere.

The cast ewe has been left
with her swollen stomach
unable to lift herself out of sleep.

But,
when morning comes
we will all be alive again.
Re born-
Dusk's pervasive prescience momentarily
rolling around in a glass jar.

Emily King is a writer, dance teacher, choreographer, and dachshund wrangler living in the Bay Area. Through both language and movement, she aims to "pour hot magic into spaces chilled with disbelief." She infuses her craft with eco-feminist themes and the whimsy she draws from her two daughters and her experiences teaching at an all-girls high school. Learn more at bit.ly/EmilyAKing and follow her on TikTok @twodachshundkings.

Category Winner:
Self-Portrait as Frida Kahlo's Flower of Life On My First Motherless Mother's Day
by Jennifer Grant

I paint flowers so they will not die ~ Frida Kahlo

I'm Frida's ember-hued fire flower—
Swaddled in lightning.

Sunburst-of-a-first-born-child,
graced with Momma's unbending will.
I'm Mandragora officinarum,
ever-blooming in poison-barbs of silence.

My roots, five decades laced
with Momma's healing-salve-love.
Today, I crave maternal tending.
My leaves wrinkly and brown,
I hug only groundcover.

No longer a daughter,
child without mother or father.
I've ceased blossoming,
not even seasonally with my sister.

In dormancy, my quiet-quills
prickle and stab at chatty trespassers.

Maybe if I transplant myself in sandy soil,
I will root-rearrange, cluster or reharmonize—
Recluse of a mandrake who shrieks
a glass-shattering-cry each night.

Jennifer Grant is not any type of flower, though she likes to periodically pretend she's as stoic as a southern magnolia or as rare as a ghost orchid. Her second collection of poetry, *Dangerous Women*, won the 2021 Blue Light Press Book Award and her first collection of poetry, *Good Form*, was published by Negative Capability Press in 2017. Her latest collection, *Flower of Life (In Three Movements)* is slated for 2026. She lives in Newberry, Florida. Keep up with her at JenniferLynnGrant.com.

What the River Knows
by Grace Yang

The river does not confess.
Its mouth full of loquat seeds and
things too smooth to name.

It carries them belly-up,
hair snagged on reeds—
a drift of wrists,
a temple charm turned over in silt.

A mother kneels at the edge,
thumbs crusted with ginger juice.
She asks in the old dialect.
The water lifts its hem,
soaks her sleeves,
does not answer.

By morning, a lacquered hush.
Fish bones caught in the throat of light.
No ripple, no song.
Only the hush that knows
what it cannot return.

Grace Yang is a Boston-based writer and poet whose work explores identity, memory, and the intersections of culture and place. Her writing has appeared or is forthcoming in local newspapers, *The Stanford Daily*, *Evanescent Magazine*, and more. Yang shares her work and connects with readers on Instagram @slicedandpitted. She is passionate about crafting stories that linger in the imagination and spark conversation.

The Shape of Your Indent
by Hannah Watson

You lay next to me all night
in the queen-sized bed, never
reaching over. I felt the weight

of your breath, the pull
of your indent in the mattress, our shared
blanket wrapped me in comfort
and questions all while keeping
a safe distance. Is this

cheating? If
we're not touching? If
we just lie here in the darkness? If
my husband has already left me
a hundred times without me knowing? Would
following the lantern of your presence, would
tracing the lines around your eyes with my fingers, would
diving into the harbor of your chest make me
the kind of disaster I'd been trying
to escape? That night

you gave me the choice
I didn't know I was making, in the hurricane
of divorce and single-parenting, you offered me
a path to a sunlit pasture, shaded spot
by the river where we could lie shoulder
to shoulder. That night, you showed me
some hands don't take.

So how could I not but sidle up
to you like a toddler, overwhelmed, seeking
shelter. It wasn't fair, I should never
have put that on you. But there
you stayed, hand raised, volunteering
an answer. All I had to do
was call on you. Of course,

I never
knew it. Didn't do it. In the morning we climbed out
separate sides, turned on the lights, straightened
the bedding with pleasantries and pauses you held
the door of my parked vehicle before you turned, hands

in pockets, towards your old blue Bronco. I never
moved my eyes from your soft stretched flannel
shoulders retreating up the sidewalk as I shifted gears,
pressed the pedal. Did you know

all along I was yours
for the taking? Did you know
I was frozen, that I would come
to regret it? Well,

I do. And I don't
for the happiness you've created
with other people in other places you've found
your own shaded grasses, a porch swing
by the lake where you listen to the tree frogs
on a slow southern evening. I'm glad.
Really. You deserve it. But

still, some nights I listen
to your music on YouTube, curl up
in the thread count of your singing, your guitar
spreads a blanket in this candlelit corner
where I sidle up alone but not
lonely. I reach over

and trace the shape
of your indent.

Hannah Watson lives in Atlanta, Georgia, where she works in the legal field. When not writing, she trains for half-marathons, stress bakes, and reads the multiplying stack of fiction overwhelming her living room bookshelves. Keeping her company in these endeavors (except the endurance running) is her pug Sherman, who claims to be her first proofreader and biggest fan. Connect with Hannah (and Sherman) on Instagram @hmewpoetry.

The Ketamine Lessons: Lesson the 83rd
by Janine Inez

The girl who climbed onto her tiny balcony and fell asleep
in the middle of winter in an attempt to freeze to death
or find The Greater Sky.
She is also you.
The girl who crawled under the table and carved cries for
help into her arms, wondering if anyone would notice
if she stayed under there forever.
She is also you.
The girl who fell in love with another girl
and fell flat on her face,
love pouring out of her eyes and ears and nose and mouth
until she nearly asphyxiated.
She is also you.
The girl who stood in front of the train turnstile crying,
Heart pulsing, terrified what she would do
if she got close to the tracks.
So strangers walking by just stopped and prayed.
She is also you.
The girl who decided she could find meaning in life again
by editing films and writing screenplays.
So she taught herself how first,
and then she went across the country to be taught.
She is also you.
The girl who went across the country to be taught writing
and got a course in mistakes (and miracles!), instead.
She is also you.
The girl who fell in and out of sanity and happiness as often
as the sun and the moon dip below the equator.
She is also you.
The girl who ricocheted back and forth
in every romantic relationship
she was lucky enough to find.
The girl who could fall in love with almost anyone.
She is also you.
The girl who barely slept, barely ate, barely breathed
for a quantity of nearly two years,
wondering if she lay still in her dorm,
very, very still, and closed her eyes
could she will her organs to stop working?
She is also you.

The girl who nearly dropped out of school,
who curled up at her childhood home
under a pile of blankets for over a year
and tried to convince herself there was just no use.
She is also you.
The girl who taught herself to paint an immaculate iris using Photoshop
one that could see all and ward off evil.
She is also you.
The girl who stayed up late eating her first meal of the day—
fried chicken bites—
at midnight with her beautiful Jamaican cousin
trying not to laugh too loud
lest she wake up the whole house.
She is also you.
The girl who pulled herself up to her elbows, then
her knees, then
her feet, wobbly now but standing,
and trudged all the way back across the country
to receive the help she needed.
She is also you.
The girl who ragefully kicked over a waste bin
in her therapist's office because they'd just come in
with news of her grandmother's death,
then immediately apologized her brains out.
She is also you.
The girl who got enough help
to go back to school,
who told herself it was what Grandma would have wanted.
She is also you.
The girl who choked on Riesling nearly every night,
eyes sparkling as she watched Samurai Champloo
and halfheartedly contemplating
which ceiling fixture in her bedroom would be sturdy enough
to affix a rope to.
She is also you.
The girl who bought a seven-day candle from the witch in the apothecary
on the way to therapy,
and lit it dutifully and as instructed
in honor of her grandmother,
in honor of her love. The girl who believed.
She is also you.
The girl who sat in the audience of strangers to receive her degree a year late,
feeling all her friends had left her behind.

The girl who never forgave them.
She is also you.
The girl who pulled herself up on
her elbows,
knees, and
hands again,
who worked odd jobs she hated because
she was sure the only thing she was missing was money, stability,
discipline, self-compassion.
She is also you.
The girl who dreamed that maybe she could heal others the
way she had been healed.
She is also you.
The girl who rewrote her entire life story and ambitions
so she would never be financially destitute again.
She is also you.
The girl who dragged her feet across the country
one more time
to pursue a better education, the way
her mother crossed oceans to go to a new country
and pursue a better
life.
She is also you.
The girl who stood tall on two feet,
applied herself,
made connections,
made best friends,
fell in love,
became the President,
wrote a novel,
wrote another one,
played board games,
all while continuing to staunchly care for her mental well-being
right up to the finish line.
She is also you.
The girl who trusted herself enough to go
to the top of the mountain
and receive.
She is also you.
The girl who descended that mountain
with grace, peace, love, gratitude,
and a kindhearted vision of her past and present selves.
She is also you.

The girl who finally, finally, finally realized that yes,
Everything Will Be Okay.
She is also you.
The little girl sitting by the windowsill
in the one-bedroom apartment
in Brooklyn, NY
losing herself in stories
to feel less alone,
mesmerized
by dust motes floating in the sunlight.
Look at her.
Look at them.
They are all you.

Dr. Janine Inez is a psychiatric nurse practitioner, narrative therapist, and multidisciplinary artist whose work lives at the intersection of psychology, liberation, and artistic recovery. She holds a BFA in Writing for Screen & Television from the University of Southern California and a doctorate from Columbia University. Her portfolio includes feature screenplays, YA novels, a poetry anthology, and a non-fiction novella. She lives in Oakland, California, with her fuzzy white terrier, Luka, and is currently working on a memoir and a YA TV pilot.

Just Black Enough
by Jasmine Troutt

"Just Black enough,"
They say, like it's a compliment.
Like being "Black" has a singular definition.
Like I belong now,
In this bubble they've created
Because I'm not *too* much.
Not *too* loud.
Not *too* dark.
Not *too* threatening.
But enough.
Enough for their entertainment.
Enough to prove they're not racist
Because they have a "black friend".

I become their sun—
They orbit me when it suits them.
Let me shine at parties,
Pull me into photos,
Ask me to say the funny slang
They ridicule others for.

But when the sun sets,
When the conversation gets deeper
They turn to the moon.
Pale.
Familiar.
Quieter.
They forget I burn

They love the way I look.
Lightskin, light eyes, freckles dusting
my cheeks.
I'm black enough to make them feel cultured
But white enough to still be the standard.

They don't see me.
They see possibilities.
The best of both worlds,
A body that checks every box—
Something to admire,
But never understand

High yellow.
Redbone.
Mulatto.
Light bright.
Exotic.

Names I've been branded with–
Like warnings, like labels on a shelf.
Their way of placing me
Where I never asked to be.
Trying to simplify something
That was never complicated to me.

I am not in-between.
I am not confused.
I am not a mix of halves–
I am whole.
And that should be enough.

I am not a puzzle,
Meant to be solved
Or made to fit your idea of "blackness".

I am not your function,|
Not your evidence,
Not your orbit.

I don't shine for you.
I am the sun,
Even when you turn away.

Jasmine Simone Troutt is a young author from Montclair, New Jersey, writing stories about queer girls with sharp voices and complicated hearts. She has published two books: *Rumor Has It*, a contemporary romance, and *Proof of Life*, a collection of poetry, essays, and short fiction. When she's not drafting new manuscripts, she's studying, playing sports, or hanging out with friends. Find her on Instagram at @ jasmine.simone.t.

Like a Poem
by JB Frady

Nothing reshapes the game,
Sets kindling, stokes the flame,
Or wins hearts and stakes its claim
Like a poem.

There's naught so Napoleonic,
Whether verbose or just laconic,
Nothing so mythically iconic
As a poem.

Nothing hopelessly obscures,
Supernaturally endures,
Or lovingly assures
Like a poem.

If there's a tool to be employed
That spreads love to be enjoyed
But also hate and has destroyed,
It's a poem.

So if you trip into a poet,
Hero or villain they'll not show it,
And if you can't discern or know it,
Run.

JB Frady is a recovering perfectionist who's learned that if you dabble in enough creative endeavors, you'll be called multitalented instead of neurotic. This novelist, poet, sculptor, music creator, standup comic, and photographer worked roughly three dozen day jobs after dropping out of college twice. It's all part of an illustrious, failproof plan which should reveal itself any day now.

Cuesta Pisar la Palta
by Magalí Clazón

(*It's hard to step on the avocado*)

"Cuesta pisar la palta"
the inner voice said.
Romper. Pisar. Quebrar.
What is that?
I've never learned how to do that.
What happens if you stop loving me
when you discover
that I have the strength
to romper, pisar, quebrar?

Is it you or I
who fears the light?
Or is it the shadow
of the courage
I'm afraid to own?
But…
cuesta pisar la palta.
Can you see it?
My mind complained.
You're not in coherence
with what you say
and what you fear.

Is that fear
of the shadow of the light
just an illusion
to keep you playing small
behind the scenes
of "cuesta pisar la palta"?

Or is there, here and now,
a chance to rewrite the stories
in the mind
and begin to
romper, pisar, quebrar
the old narratives
once and for all?

Ouch.

Can I be gentler
with what I need to overcome?
Actually,
nice is what kept you behind, my doll.
Scream. Shout. Release.

Who cares who gets scared?
More will see
what you are about to become.
Burn. Burn. Burn.
The ave phoenix, said.

Poetry is made from ashes.
Keep watching the ember.
Poetry will watch you re-emerge.
Watch me, mi amor.

Magali Clazon is an Argentine poet and movement artist now creating her magic in San Francisco. Her work emerges from a deep devotion to embodiment, music, storytelling, and the unseen threads that connect body, nature, and spirit. Through somatic ritual and poetic expression, she builds spaces where others can soften, remember, and return to their inner truth. Her art invites a tender awakening of the soul's creative intelligence. Find her at MagaliClazon.com and on Instagram @ magaliclazon.

void
by Michael Miller

the void from which the universe emerged
must have bequeathed the substance of us all
when all that nothingness together splurged
to spread the stars across the evening's sprawl.
when we are born and face this grand facade
we hold faith dear and struggle to survive.
we fill the nothingness by which we're awed
with what brief hopes and dreams we can contrive.
where comes our great attempt to make some sense
as if the universe contained an order?
each day we tread along the narrow fence
of life's and death's shared incoherent border.
   the void that sits inside the heart of matter
   awaits the final pieces of life's tatter.

Michael Miller lives in Edmonds, WA, on the Puget Sound with his wife and their two cats. In 2022, Michael received an honorable mention in the Yeats Society of New York's Poetry Prize and in 2022, 2024, and 2025 he was selected as a finalist in the San Francisco Writer Contest. His poems have appeared in the New Guard Review, Lyric Magazine, and others. He received his Master's in English from SFSU from the Creative Writing Department.

Poppy Field
by Sharla Dawn

Lady Poppy pops her floppy top-mop wide open
to see love's pollen seekers, locate compassion's tickle.
In time the whole field of poppies opens orange and free.
Dizzily humming with bees and sunshine,
they roam erratic breezes until their stems
hurtle their silly heads back
for a moment. Or per-
haps sling too far,
slump
on
the
wob-
bling
shoul-
der
of
a
sis-
ter.

Sharla Dawn Robinson Ng, JD writes imaginatively, even drawing from dreams. Recent themes include transformative effects of art, lawyering with consciousness rooted in nature, living abroad in South Korea, and cultural associations with flowers. Chief editor of a 2022 anthology by the Live Poets Society, Sharla appreciates the group's give-and-take model of communication, which is based on mutual respect and honest, supportive feedback. She lives in a river valley in the northwest. SharlaDawnPoet.com

Sonnet 36
by Uncle Dom

Across the gusty deep of Time's expanse,
A distant call more faintly felt than heard.
Its message muffled by the squall's romance –
The flurry of distraction ne'er deferred.
But if attuned when source is amplified,
A moment when cacophony abates,
The resonance unmutes the voice inside.
The call then casts the tethers it creates.
Comes next the daily struggle then to bind
Those wisps into suspension ropes of skill:
The braidings made from works of heart and mind;
Diversions spurned by practiced acts of will.
   The bridge through time is built to there herefrom
   By who you are to who you might become.

Dominick fell in love with reading and writing in 2022, which began his path of creative writing. He discovered a proclivity for verse that year, and in 2025 realized that iambic pentameter was his proper form for expression. His first publication will be a collection of sonnets.

ADULT NONFICTION

Category Winner:
Indra's Net
by Indra Rinzler

In a VERY quick moment, everything changed. Life as we know it began. The Big Bang was just the first miracle. Life is a series of miracles, moment to moment.

Experience: The Universe

In his book, *A Brief History of Time,* written forty-some years ago, Stephen Hawking explains the beginning of the existence of our Universe. He says: "We can explain why the big bang occurred about ten thousand million years ago—it takes about that long for intelligent beings to evolve. An early generation of stars had to form. These stars converted some of the original hydrogen and helium into elements like carbon and oxygen, out of which we are made. The stars then exploded as supernovas, and their debris went to form other stars and planets, among them those of our solar system, which is about five thousand million years old. The first one or two thousand million years of the Earth's existence were too hot for the development of anything complicated. The remaining three thousand million years or so have been taken up by the slow process of biological evolution, which has led them from the simplest organisms to beings who are capable of measuring time back to the big bang." It took ten billion years to form our Universe and, somehow, Hawking condenses those years down to just a few simple acts—keystrokes of moments in time. The basis is high school science. Elements get changed into other elements; heat is involved.

I am impressed by how the cosmic intelligence takes care of us. It is kind of like my wife's cooking: a tomato there, a spice here, a little time, and wow, what a meal.

A few days ago, I read an online comment about how there isn't any food delivery except for pizza in my hometown in California. A user wrote that if he wants some Chinese food, "Oh well, I guess I have to go get it myself." Maybe this is an understandable complaint, but come on guys, get some perspective.

It took two billion years just to cool the planet down to livable temperatures! Let's broaden our viewpoint a bit. Let's live like this life is a miracle, which in fact it is.

I wake up in the morning. Wake up from what to what? I get hungry. What is hunger? I eat my oatmeal. It tastes so good. What is taste? How do I know what it tastes like? The food digests and feeds my body. How many cells are involved? How many chemical reactions have occurred? I notice, but I don't orchestrate; it just happens on its own.

And yet we live like life owes us what we want right here, right now.

The periodic table of elements isn't just a list of elements. It explains the alchemical-like experience of *you*! Take an element, add a neutron or proton, and poof! It is an entirely different element.

There is awe in the complete and total miracle of life. Food grows, we eat. It is digested and the body keeps functioning. We get a fresh reset each day. Our daily reset is like the ten-billion-year condensation of a living organism, the Universe, that reminds us of a presence at work in our lives.

Let each day become like a big bang to show us what a miracle life is in the Universe.

Significance: Saturn, focus, discipline, restriction, construction, seriousness, details, completion, releasing old karma, self-knowledge, wheel of life, unification, responsibility

Lessons: The most basic lesson of life applies here: As above, so below. The completion of life's cycle is to see the large and the small as the same. Life happens for us, not to us. The simplest of truths, like how ants support each other, can be the key to opening to the highest joy.

Practices: Actively feel gratitude for everything that comes in a day. Find a place where you can observe insects working. Make friends with the resistances you face in your life.

Next Step: Work on trusting and accepting what is instead of asking for more.

Contemplate: All the bodily and natural functions that happen on their own without you having to think about them or do anything.

Higher Octave: Freedom from *burdensome* responsibility.

Affirmation: The Universe and I are One.

Indra Rinzler is a lifetime spiritual seeker and has been studying astrology and spirituality for more than 50 years. He offers life readings for clients using Vedic astrology, the Enneagram of Personality, and Astrocartography. Indra aims to help people live in the moment, beyond their conditioned stories. He writes, teaches, heals, and counsels, and is a frequent guest on podcasts. Indra's Net is his first book. You can learn more about him and his work at IndraRinzler.com

Changing Woman Speaks:
From Lost to Found in the Navajo Beauty Way
by Brenda Kay Beck

CHAPTER ONE: *Between Two Worlds*

The Phoenix sky is dark and ominous as I step out of the airport terminal and climb into the front seat of the car beside the Navajo medicine man. Great jagged streaks of searing white lightning tear across the heavens and slash down to the earth in every direction. They are relentless and all around us as we head north out of Phoenix towards Flagstaff and the Rez.

As many times as I've been to Phoenix, nothing seems familiar. The lightning is disorienting, and he's driving on back roads to avoid the rush hour traffic. I'm in his territory now, and this Navajo man, whom I've known for several years, is taking me somewhere way up north tonight to the Navajo Indian Reservation, where he's going to sneak me into a private ceremony.

Just an hour ago, I was on a plane flying in from New York, having spent a week with the editors of Reader's Digest in our corporate headquarters north of Manhattan. Three other top advertising sales executives and I had been chosen from our New York, Detroit, Chicago, and West Coast offices to be immersed in the magazine's unique editorial process while honing our own editing skills.

I'd spent this morning working on our final assignment in a private office, sitting at an antique French writing desk and gazing at a lovely painting of ballerinas hanging on the wall in front of me. Suddenly, I realized it was an original Degas, and I was sitting at the desk of Lila Wallace, Reader's Digest's beloved co-founder, art collector, and philanthropist. I was in the presence of beauty, and Mrs. Wallace's legacy inspired me to do my very best work.

My colleagues and I had been given one hour to edit a nine-page Newsweek article down to one and a half pages for Reader's Digest. The editor apologized as he hustled us off to private offices, saying, "It's an impossible task in an hour, but please do the best you can."

Exactly one hour later, a senior editor reviewed my work and was thrilled that I'd nearly replicated, word-for-word, his own edit of the same article which was about to be published. News of my achievement quickly circulated the hallowed offices, and I was patted on the back and told they would hire me on the spot if I were applying for an editor's job. It was obvious they hadn't expected this from an advertising salesperson. It had been a good week for me, and I would be remembered for it.

I bid farewell to my colleagues at noon and climbed into the Lincoln Town Car that would take me to John F. Kennedy Airport. I had less than an hour to figure out a wardrobe change from my corporate suit and heels to a Navajo ceremonial outfit, whatever that might look like. On the way to the airport, my driver waited for me at the White Plains shopping mall while I tore through the racks looking for something that would work. Thirty minutes later I emerged wearing a calf-length, tiered denim skirt, a western-style blouse, and a tooled leather belt which paired with the boots I had worn to New York. I told the salesgirl I was headed to Arizona, and she envisioned me at a fancy dude ranch. *That's close enough*, I thought to myself as I hustled out.

In the car, I plaited my long brown hair into a single French braid down my back. I'd read that traditional Navajo women don't leave their long hair hanging loose but arrange it in a special bun. The braid was my effort to be respectful, and it was the best I could do in a pinch.

Before my plane took off, I left a message for my best friend back in San Francisco saying where I was going and with whom. Without this call, no one would ever know I'd changed my flight to land in Phoenix and would soon be somewhere deep in the native lands of northern Arizona. My voicemail ended with, "If I don't call you by Sunday evening, I want you to know where I was last headed and with whom!"

Five hours later, my plane dropped down through the altitude levels into a different climate, a different culture, and a totally different reality. As we taxied to the gate, I tried to prepare myself for what I'd signed up for. I wasn't scared, but very excited with a million questions. This wasn't another Navajo workshop but the real deal, a chance to visit the Navajo Reservation with my teacher, Robert Preston, and attend a traditional ceremony. I wasn't going to miss it for the world, as I might never have another opportunity to do this.

I met Robert three years ago in Nine Gates Mystery School, a spiritual retreat program in northern California which focused on the chakras, the nine energy centers of the body. The teachers were international shamans and priests who shared their traditional teachings, songs, and ceremonies in weekend intensives. When the program ended that year, some of us were drawn to Robert and his Native American ways, so we sponsored him to come back to California once a month to teach us.

He was introduced to us as a full-blooded Navajo medicine man who was raised in Tuba City, Arizona, a small town on the western side of the Navajo Indian Reservation near the Grand Canyon. His father was a decorated Navajo Code Talker in World War II. His paternal grandfather was the first Vice Chairman of the Navajo Nation and a formidable Navajo medicine man himself. Robert's teachings run deep, and he has helped a lot of people through his traditional ways.

I was surprised to learn that he's also a college-educated businessman. When I met him, he was working for a large financial services company in Phoenix. Now he lives in Flagstaff, Arizona, where he owns a computer consulting business and a Chinese restaurant on the Reservation. He opened the restaurant over a year ago to provide work for his son, his eldest daughter, and her partner, who is a Chinese chef.

Peking Gardens was a success the moment it opened in Tuba City. The Chinese food was excellent and the only game in town aside from the Navajo tacos and burger stand across the street from the gas station. It was full every night and his family were having fun running it, until things started to implode.

One weekend, the chef flew back to San Francisco's Chinatown to visit his family and mysteriously disappeared. Personal cell phones were not a thing yet, so no one could reach him. Six weeks passed before he was able to relay a message back through a friend. Evidently, his traditional Chinese parents didn't think too highly of their first-born son being with a native woman, and they had no intention of letting him return to Arizona. Never mind that the young couple had a baby on the way. That probably made it worse. He was essentially kidnapped, and it was clear he wouldn't be back. Ever.

With the chef gone and the staff devastated, the sous chef stepped in and did a great job replicating the traditional Chinese dishes. But the business was bleeding money. Robert combed through the finances, spent time in the restaurant and interviewed the staff, but couldn't figure out the problem. Then bizarre car accidents started happening in rapid succession with different family members in the restaurant's parking lot.

I was in New York when Robert called to tell me he'd hired a medicine man for a reading. The medicine man had consulted his crystals and said there was black magic involved and that a protection ceremony was needed as soon as possible. It was scheduled for this weekend, the weekend I was flying home from New York.

I jumped at the chance to be invited. Robert was my spiritual teacher, but we had also become business confidants. He'd been talking about his restaurant problems for months, so I knew the issues and how precarious things were. I wanted to support him, and really wanted to see the ceremony.

Back in my New York hotel room at the end of my day, Robert calls to explain that this will be a private ceremony without his family or the restaurant staff. It will just be him and the medicine man. But I plead my case hard, coming from the place of supportive friend and colleague, while trying not to sound too pushy. It will be so easy for me to stop in Phoenix on the way home, so I feel like it's a sign I should be there. Finally, he relents and invites me. He says if I can swing the layover, he'll pick me up at the Phoenix airport and we'll drive up together.

So that's how I got here, fresh off the plane from New York, and heading into the unknown. Was I crazy to come? Probably. I could be home right now, relaxing from my long week with a glass of wine. Maybe the better question is, "What have I gotten myself into, and will I be safe?" But I have a trusted guide so I shouldn't be worried. Right?

Brenda Kay Beck is an award-winning author, film producer, and practitioner of the Navajo Beauty Way. At the height of her professional career, she married a Navajo medicine man and began a lifelong quest to understand and follow the teachings of this rich Native American culture. She is passionate about helping preserve their sacred stories and share why they are so relevant and important in these changing times. Her books and films can be found at BrendaKayBeck.com.

Nasty Eggs
by Chris Zamani

*"I wanted you to be able to talk to anyone, from the poor and hopeless to kings
and presidents, so I had to show you people living at their lowest." - Mom*

Mom created opportunities for her children to gain perspective and appreciate the struggles of others. Before our family would need to dine at soup kitchens for our own sustenance, Mom brought us one afternoon to have a meal at the Poverello House, a homeless shelter. Inside the large cafeteria, were long parallel rows of tables and benches where people ate side by side. The air in the shared space was stale, a melange of mildew, sweat, and cigarette smoke mingled with the umami scents wafting from chafing trays full of food.

Mom held my youngest sister, Kiara, in her arms and led the way as my sister Brittany, brother Marcus, and I, entered the line together. Each of us took a partitioned food tray as we shuffled along the serving line. At each station, a volunteer unceremoniously dolloped a serving spoonful into each respective well of the rectangular tray: corn, peas, beef stroganoff and fruit cocktail. A small plastic tumbler of fruit punch completed the meal, and we shimmied between the tightly spaced rows of tables to find some unoccupied bench space where we could all sit and eat as a family.

Looking around, I witnessed the gaze of hundreds of eyes cast downward. People sat with their necks bent deeply as if their chins were tethered to their chests. Maybe it was for necessity to facilitate the efficient shoveling of food into hungry mouths, maybe it was not the slouched kyphosis of broken spirits. For a dining hall holding hundreds of people, there was remarkably little conversation. A few hushed tones droned in the background, subsumed by the scraping sounds of forks on teeth, the scratching of spoons on plastic trays, and a cacophony of slurps, gulps, sniffles, and coughs.

An emotional collage of disgust, embarrassment, and pity formed patterns in my thoughts like a kaleidoscope of grim reflections. I felt like I wanted to create distance between myself and the other diners. I knew that our reality as a family was precariously close to everyone else in that hall. I harbored a kernel of resentment against the people surrounding me. I was weighted by the sense of despair and circumstantial permanence that seemed to exude from the faces and bodies of many of those with whom we shared the meal. I felt the void of abdicated dreams and lives surrendered to fate.

***

In 1993, we spent a week at the emergency family shelter just around the corner from the Poverello House. We hadn't lost our home—our refrigerator had. After our old fridge broke a few months earlier, Mom had gotten a new one from a rent-to-own store, and when she fell behind on payments, the company came to repossess it.

She cried when the truck arrived at our house to take the refrigerator back. Pleas to allow her to keep the refrigerator for the sake of her four children did not move the workers to risk their own livelihood by defying the directive of their boss to reappropriate the property which Mom had stopped making payments on. Initially, all of our food went into a large ice chest, yet after a few days Mom accepted that she could not safely keep food stored like that, nor could she afford the cost of constantly buying ice and losing the savings from no longer purchasing food in bulk.

The emergency family shelter was a converted motel. There were two stories of single rooms with attached bathrooms. Inside the room was a queen bed, two twins, and a small refrigerator. A single small wooden cross adorned the sterile white walls of the room. Marcus and I each slept on a twin bed while Mom shared the queen with Brittany and Kiara.

The former motel lobby now served as a common room stocked with board games and a chalkboard where staff led mandatory Bible lessons. Each day, the PA system announced the start of Bible study, its crackling voice carrying through every hallway and room in the facility. Unlike in years past, when we still went to church, I had the wherewithal to not ask challenging questions or look a gift horse in the mouth by showing my annoyance at being proselytized as a condition for receiving assistance.

The parking lot had been converted into a playground with a sandbox, a few tricycles, and a seesaw that gave me and my siblings some joyous moments, though at thirteen I felt far too old to be enjoying such childish pastimes. I could tell that Mom was stressed, but she wasn't defeated.

What started as a single meal at the Poverello House —previously for the purpose of providing a lesson in perspective and empathy—became our regular source for breakfast and dinner; lunch was usually tuna sandwiches or peanut butter and jelly that we kept in the small fridge in our room.

Unlike the previous field trip to the Poverello House, this time I noticed a man who sat with an upright posture and ate with his head aloft. A Black man with dark hair on the sides, bald on the top, and a full beard that he kept neatly groomed with a slight shimmer that let me know he had applied some hair oils and cared for his hygiene. He was also there with his family, but I do not remember them; his was the presence that left an impression. He sat across from us one morning and stared at me with amusement as I ate around my scrambled eggs.

After a few minutes he asked, "Why don't you eat your eggs? They make you strong!"

"Uhhh, because it's the unborn fetus of a chicken," I replied.

"Yeah!" Marcus cosigned, as he also was never a fan of eggs—an aversion I grew out of, but he still retains to this day.

"Let me get some of that fetus," he said, reaching across the table without so much as a request for permission. He skewered the overcooked, solid cake of scrambled egg with his fork and lifted it, jiggling, across the table to his tray. He smiled at me as he put the entire mass of yellow flubber into his mouth and chewed with an exaggerated mastication of his jaw. "Mmmm, that's some good fetus!" he said after partially swallowing.

I cracked an entertained grimace of disgust and coaxed out an "ughhh" under my breath in response. He gave me a wink, and I continued to eat the rest of my breakfast, quietly grateful that he had taken the nasty eggs off my plate but also feeling appreciative at his display of humanity and self-pride—unhindered by his presence in that soul-draining circumstance with his family.

Chris Zamani is a physician and writer whose work bridges medicine, identity, and the search for meaning. His life and career have taken him across five countries, reflecting a commitment to healing both the body and the spirit. He writes about belonging, liberation, and the quiet transformations that emerge through struggle. Learn more at ChrisZamani.com.

Midnight Mantras
by Chris Zamani

My earliest memory is of the inside of a windowless hospital room. The walls were light mustard yellow. To the left of me was a hospital gurney where my brother Marcus sat up watching me. Grandma sat in a chair watching the both of us. I was dancing and singing to the tune of Jingle Bells:

"Sickle cell, sickle cell, sickle all the way.

"Oh what fun it is to ride with sickle cell today, HEY!"

Marcus cracked a half-amused, half-annoyed grimace as he looked at me, his left forearm taped to a padded armboard meant to keep his wrist straight, preventing kinks in the line tethering him to the IV pole. Grandma looked down at me with the slightly amused absent gaze I would later come to recognize as the expression she used to put emotional distance between herself and the moment.

I must've been about three years old at the time.

Marcus was born with sickle cell anemia, an inherited disease where red blood cells can distort into crescent shapes—like a sickle's blade—then snag in small vessels and block blood flow, starving tissues of oxygen. The result is what we call a sickle cell crisis. It causes tissue damage. It causes pain. Sometimes it means medication. Sometimes it means the hospital.

Marcus is fifteen months older than me. We're so close in age that, in our early years, people often mistook us for twins. We were playmates, roommates, friends at times, and enemies other times.. Together we planned and plotted how to build airplanes out of cardboard to fly away and made satellite dishes with aluminum foil to pick up cable TV stations.

In earlier times, before the birth of my younger sisters, when it was just Marcus, Mom and me, there was an innocence and sense of wonder that painted most of my days with awe. I remember the smell of seawater at El Segundo Beach and the excitement of going to Grandma's house. Pain was already a part of my consciousness, but it did not occupy the majority of my thoughts and experiences.

Sickle cell was there, it was always there, but it was a beast I was still largely shielded from. I remember hospital rooms, stuffed animals, ice cream cups with small wooden spoons, and play rooms staffed by hospital volunteers. I remember the smell of latex and Lysol and stale urine inside of bedside urinals. But at this point in life, I was still protected from the worst.

Mom would bring me to the hospital to visit Marcus in his recovery, after the most terrifying moments had passed. I had yet to see the emergency rooms and the blood draws, had not yet witnessed nurses holding Marcus down to insert IV lines and the helpless sobbing of my mother. The stage of fear and powerlessness would come a few years later.

***

Sickle cell is a thief. A lurking entity that could hide for long periods of time and then violate my sense of safety and normalcy just as I let my guard down. Growing up watching Marcus, I was always waiting for the other shoe to drop.

Marcus could go months without pain and then suddenly have a major crisis and suffer daily. There seemed to be no pattern, rhyme, or reason. Exercise, a viral infection, an asthma attack, high-altitude environments, and emotional distress could trigger a sickle cell crisis, or it could occur with no identifiable triggers at all.

As a kid, Marcus was an emotional juggernaut. His anger was omnipresent. There was inherent cruelty in the world for Marcus, growing up under the threat of physical torture that could arise at any time. Not only was there a struggle with pain, fatigue, and weakness, but there was also the battle against the adults whom he fought, quite literally tooth and nail, in emergency bays and hospital rooms. Marcus was angry at his body, the pain he experienced, the doctors and nurses, and Mom for taking him into healthcare settings where he felt a lack of bodily autonomy.

As any parent who has taken their child to get a vaccination can attest, fearful kids can muster incredible strength to avoid a needle poke. Later in my life, while on pediatric rotations during residency training, I came to understand the need to restrain young children so that, as healthcare professionals, we could safely perform the pokes and prods inherent to modern medical practice. Yet despite how common scared kids are, and the skill pediatric nurses develop at holding them still, I would never in my career witness the anger and intensity I saw in Marcus as he fought the adults who denied him sovereignty over his body. It impacted me deeply, but nothing influenced my life trajectory more profoundly than watching Marcus in pain.

***

The most intense crises peaked in the middle of the night. Sure, there were always the moments watching Marcus walk slowly away from the playground, or noticing as he would rhythmically rub his knee with the palm of his hand while sitting watching TV, or the silence that would replace laughter, signaling me that there was pain brewing. But it was after dark, after I had fallen asleep, that the pattern of powerlessness and fear would express itself in recurrent episodes.

My eyelids would part to the sounds of Marcus suffering. I could gauge the intensity of the episode based on how he cried. There was the moan—deep, closed mouth bellows that seemed to come from his chest—repeating every second or two in a series of 8-10, punctuated with a guttural hiss through parted lips. This meant that a trip to the emergency room was coming. I would climb down from the top bunk, the grogginess of disrupted sleep mixing with a pressure behind my eyes that I came to associate with fear and a warmth in my chest that I now understand as a somatic expression of deep sadness.

I would go get a laundry basket, inside which I would place a towel, a blanket and school clothes for the next morning, and prepare to carry this care package to Rose's house. Rose was our next-door neighbor, a retired woman who must've been in her late sixties. She reminded me of Grandma. Her house was always clean and uncluttered. She didn't even have roaches, though from time to time she would complain that when we set off bug bombs, our roaches would come hide at her house. She often watched my sisters and me while Mom would pack up with Marcus and head into the emergency room at Valley Children's Hospital.

Midnight trips to the E.R. were not the only way pain haunted our nights. Sometimes the moaning was less intense. A droning sound that escaped from his quasi-sleeping level of consciousness. A dream state auditory protest to the antics that his body was putting him through, seemingly not enough to awaken him fully, but enough to keep me just shy of the transition to slumber. I would lay there feeling the frustration of time that slowed down and made minutes feel like journeys of perseverance unto themselves.

Other times, I would awaken to Marcus screaming. His pain was so intense that all he could do to cope in the moment was to force as much air as possible from his lungs, through his vocal cords and out into the atmosphere of our shared bedroom. I want to believe that at some level it helped him deal with the intensity of the pain, as if each decibel carried away the energy of the torment from his body. In these moments, there was no fog of sleepiness, only a wide-eyed alertness, and the chest warmth of sadness ascending to my throat so that I could swallow it down to prevent myself from crying. I would hold the tears from falling as the pressure in the corners of my eyes gave me a stuffy nose.

The worst experience came when the screaming stopped. Many have witnessed a child cry so hard that no sound escapes as they choke on shallow breaths for a few seconds until a loud wail can escape their throat. When his pain was at its worst, Marcus could not make a sound. A silent open-mouthed suspended breath, punctuated by short, shallow inhalations that would convulse his body out of its rigid fetal position for a brief second before curling back as if to protect his core from a kick to the ribs. In these moments, fear gripped my body in a tense suspended animation. The subtle tremble of my jaw created a soft clatter of my back teeth. Shallow breaths and racing heartbeats structured short mantras of prayers to God, composing a melody of powerless desperation.

Chris Zamani is a physician and writer whose work bridges medicine, identity, and the search for meaning. His life and career have taken him across five countries, reflecting a commitment to healing both the body and the spirit. He writes about belonging, liberation, and the quiet transformations that emerge through struggle. Learn more at ChrisZamani.com.

Lost and Found,
Prologue of Seven Stitches in Neverland:
A Daughter, Her Homeless Mother, and the
Peter Pan Costumes that Mended the Past
by Donna Stevens Kehl

The gravel crunched under my tender bare feet with each new step, and several loose pebbles embedded into the soft crevices between my toes. It was still dark out on that damp, foggy morning, and I had nowhere to go and no one to turn to, for I had committed an unthinkable crime. Ordered out of the warmth of the house, and out into the cool, damp morning air, I crossed the gravel driveway in nothing but my pee-soaked underwear and my tiny white t-shirt. "Pee-pots cannot live in this house, get out!" ordered my mother as she slammed the door behind me.

With this revelation, my tears streamed like tiny icicles down my cheeks. I crossed that gravel driveway and sat on the icy steel tailgate of my dad's old Chevy pickup. The dampness of my pea-soaked underwear caused my skin to stick to the frosty metal. I sat there crying in the cold, and with each little sob, I blew out a little warm puff of exhaled air.

Goosebumps covered my body, and my fingers began to turn blue from the cold. I cried for what seemed like an eternity as headlights shining down my street signaled that I was not alone. A blue Ford Pinto approached in the fog, and the car slowed as it drove past my house. I hugged my body and shivered, shrinking with stinging shame as the unknown driver turned his head to stare at me as he drove past my house. I wondered if the driver was surprised to see me sitting outside alone in the wee hours of a chilly, September morning.

Sitting in the cold, my body was freezing on the outside as my heart was freezing on the inside. I was freezing and shutting out the wickedness of the woman who was my mother. Her warmth and hugs after I had served the duration of my punishment would be futile, as the damage had been done. There would be more days like this to come, but on this day, I was five years old, and it was to be my first day of kindergarten.

It's odd to think of this now, thirty-nine years later, as I pull up next to the trash bin next to the Dollar Store. Maybe it was the crunch of the gravel under my tires that triggered the memory. The crunch had echoed and reverberated as I maneuvered my car to a stop. Dazed and tired from the eight-hour drive, I sat in my car for a few moments before getting out to face the unknown. Lucky for me, I had three days off from teaching due to the President's Day holiday. Frank and Michael had stayed home as Michael had a play date, and Frank needed to get some writing done for his freelancing job, which was turning out to be quite promising.

"I'll clean this mess up when I get home," I called out to my husband on my way out the door.

Costumes and sketches were laid out on the kitchen table for *Peter Pan*, and piles of fabric filled the adjacent living room like fabric cairns in every corner. The auditions would start on Tuesday, after the long weekend, and my mind was filled with all the things I needed to do to get ready. I needed to print out monologues and cast contracts for my actors and check on the shipment of scripts. I needed to contact the drama teacher at the high school to recruit peer buddies to come over to help coach my kids on some improvisation and acting techniques.

The kids had voted on Peter Pan. Deep down inside, I worried about how I was going to get Peter Pan to fly, and I was feeling sort of lost.

Ha! That's funny! I'm a lost Boy, or a lost girl. I am a lost woman.

Ok, that is a lie, I am not a lost woman. I am a found woman, I found myself a long time ago, way before I ever dreamed of parking next to this dumpster next to the Dollar store in Redding, California, because of something deep inside me that I can't explain.

I should turn around and go back home, but I am an honorable person. I am successful, I am secure, I'm married, I have a life. Nothing can hurt me right now. She can't hurt me now. I am brave. I am fierce. I am a warrior.

I am not lost.

I opened the car door and stepped barefoot onto the gravel driveway next to the dumpster that is next to the Dollar store. I had taken my shoes off in the car.

That was stupid, I thought.

I wiped away a few pieces of gravel that had stuck between my toes before putting my shoes on, and I slowly walked towards a worn path behind the store.

I walked on, crunching through the gravel, and the sound of the gravel triggered a feeling of fear and isolation from my childhood. I felt like the little girl stuck and frozen to the back of my dad's steel tailgate, waiting for my punishment to end.

I could turn back right now and drive back home RIGHT NOW, I thought. *I don't need to do this,* but I crunched on through the gravel to the worn tire-rutted path behind the store.

Next to the path rutted with deep wheel marks, a giant Food for Less shopping cart overflowed with stuffed black plastic bags. I surveyed the rutted path, the gravel, the patches of grass, and the alley behind the store. I scanned a neglected tree adorned with a few clinging yellow leaves.

Spring is coming, little tree; all hope is not lost. Maybe someday soon you will blossom. Yet, you are a pitiful, neglected tree. Maybe you will languish there alone.

Past the tree was a loading dock at the back of the store. There was a giant refrigerator box laid down on its side, draped with a thick brown insulated blanket. Inside the box was a cozy pad of blankets. It looked surprisingly comfortable and warm. I then took a deep breath and crouched down to match the posture of the woman sitting cross-legged in the opening of the insulated refrigerator box. She looked different. Her feet were stuffed into tiny black shoes that looked too small for her feet.

The woman wore her long white hair in a topknot on the top of her head, and she was dressed in black leggings and a black sweatshirt. She rubbed her eyes and yawned, and it seemed that the noise of my car had woken her.

I crouched down and peered into the woman's icy steel eyes, which were as cold as that September day when I was five, and said, "Hello, Mother. I've been looking for you."

Dr. Donna Stevens Kehl, Ed.D., is a Drama, English, and Special Education teacher whose work appears in Story Summit's *We See You, We Hear You* anthology. Her debut memoir, *Seven Stitches in Neverland*, chronicles rescuing her estranged mother from homelessness while directing *Peter Pan the Musical*, braiding themes of trauma, reconciliation, and intergenerational healing. Through her storytelling, Donna illuminates the complexities of homelessness, family estrangement, and the redemptive power of creativity and forgiveness. Learn more at DonnaStevensKehl. com.

Menopause Showdown
by Laura O. Bergman

I'm in Newport Beach, Orange County. I'm driving down this cute little shopping street, looking for my morning coffee because I'm in dire need of caffeine at 11 am on a weekday, as one is when one has recently become an empty nester. I spot the most perfect space on the corner, right in front of the cafe I like. So I slow down, and I realize pretty quickly that it's not really a spot, it's right behind a crosswalk, but it's ok, there's enough space for me, and I'm only running in for a minute, right? I pull in, start backing up so that I'm not blocking the crosswalk, checking my rear-view camera the whole time, and a HONK comes from behind me. I can see in my camera that I still have like two feet, so I ignore it and keep going for a sec to straighten out. HOOONK!!! Longer this time. I stop and pull up to make sure the crazy person behind me knows I'm not dinging their car. I'm driving a nice new car, so do they not realize new cars all have rear-view cameras?? What the fuck. I open my door and start making my way to the sidewalk when I see the honker behind the wheel, a woman in a giant behemoth of a car. She rolls down the window and shouts out, "THAT'S NOT A PARKING SPOT! THAT. IS. NOT. A PARKING SPOT!!" Her grayish blonde hair is piled up on top of her head and is bobbing up and down violently as she shrieks, and her tan face is all askew. The anger is hissing out of her. It's all a bit much given the circumstances. So what do I do? Well, I should have ignored her and kept moving, but I just don't like being assaulted by an angry stranger for no good reason. So I engage, as one does, and I say in a smart-ass tone, "I'm only running in to grab coffee!" And then of course I have to add, for good measure, "By the way, I could see exactly how close I was to your car, I obviously have a rearview camera." Duh. I'm stoking the fire now. She screams, I mean screams, "TOO CLOSE!!! YOU. WERE. TOO. CLOSE!!!!!!".

Menopause is a bitch.

I realized later that I should have recognized her behavior, since it mirrored mine before I got help. I'd had similar instances of unhinged rage and other pesky symptoms, and eventually talked to my doctor about it.

My doctor referred me to a gynecologist who specializes in hormone replacement therapy, inserting pellets subcutaneously in a woman's backside. I went to see her and she laid out her rote speech, "It's perfectly safe… the old school medical field, i.e., male doctors, said HRT caused cancer, blah blah blah… it was a flawed study. Now. Lower your undies, and let's get to it."

The first week after my procedure, I felt a big change in my mood. The gynecologist had told me that I'd feel the burst of testosterone in the pellet, but that it would protect my mind from developing dementia so I thought, great—let's go. And the next few days I noticed my volatile mood–anger suddenly flaring up for no real reason. I was snapping at my husband for every annoying little thing he did. And there were many, many annoying little things he did.

At the same time, my libido was waking up—yawning and stretching, like after a long nap. More like a winter's hibernation, you could say. I was suddenly noticing the hot men in commercials. The fit men jogging by as I walked my dog. The handsome weatherman on the news. Heck, even my mailman wasn't safe from my ogling. I had mom-porn fantasies—a gorgeous shirtless man vacuuming the house while cooking dinner for me.

The good news was, I had a perfectly good man at home. One who would love and appreciate this new me. But his annoying little habits were really getting under my skin. I was horny, but I was too annoyed to want to have sex with him.

The weirdest part of the whole situation was, it felt as though the emotional side of my brain, let's call it the "feminine side," was shut off. Sometimes he would talk about his feelings, and I genuinely wouldn't understand what he was saying. In my mind, I was checking the score of the game. And I don't even watch sports.

Yadda yadda yadda is what I heard. Whine, whine, whine is what I picked up. I started noticing that when I watched a movie, like say a romcom, I wasn't paying attention to the dialogue or the story plot. I was looking at the beautiful people instead, and imagining them naked. Holy shit, I thought, I have become a dude!

It was such an enlightening perspective on being a man. These male "creatures" suddenly made much more sense to me. They want less talk and more action, I get it!

About two weeks into the treatment, I felt absolutely euphoric. My brain was zinging like never before. I actually remembered what a charged proton was when my son asked me one day for a school assignment. My body felt like perfection; my self-confidence soared. I thought, so this is why women do hormone replacement therapy! I feel amazing!

This happiness lasted for about two days. Then it started wearing off, and my old self came slinking back. My brain was back to not remembering what I did last weekend, let alone what a charged proton was.

I called my primary doctor and described the whole episode to her. She was at a loss, as was I. She said, "Well, I guess it's not for you." Yeah, I agreed. Oh well.

So naturally, I went back and tried the pellet insertion one more time, as one does. I mean, those two days where I felt like I owned the world? I'd do anything to have that feeling back. I thought, "Maybe it was just a bad batch?" You know how we women do that. We do the same with bad relationships. We tell ourselves, "he'll change once we're married!" We just can't get enough of torturing ourselves.

Unfortunately, I felt the same the second time around. Oh, hello old friend, I said to the mirror when its reflection couldn't grasp what my husband was whining about... Something about me not being sensitive to his feelings or some other blah blah. I was already scanning the TV for a Gillette for Men commercial.

After that, I learned my lesson. I gave up the pellets. I became my old sensitive self again. The world was back in its natural order. Yes, I felt a little older, but also a little wiser, a little more compassionate, and a little less of a dick. I appreciate that my husband is still nice to me, watches sitcoms for the actual story and not just the beautiful people, and mostly listens to what I'm saying. And vice versa.

Now, that doesn't mean I don't sometimes act like a smart-ass when an unhinged woman honks at me before my morning coffee, but these days I'm more inclined just to let her blow off steam, and I refrain from yelling back, knowing how much menopause sucks.

Laura Bergman is a nonprofit leader who has spent more than twenty-five years crafting stories to advance meaningful causes and raise millions of dollars. Since retiring in 2022, she has devoted her time to mentoring future changemakers and writing for the joy of it. Her short story *Menopause Showdown* was first published in Written Tales Magazine, and will be performed in the upcoming Menopause Monologues. Both her short story and her memoir, *Waiting for Miles*, were shortlisted by The Letter Review. Find her on Substack: @laurabergmanwrites.

Lesbian, Who Are You?
by Nikki K. Lopez

The lesbian community is filled with myths, discrimination, labels, and rules. And yet, it's also a space for love, discovery, and authenticity, if we allow it to be.

But how do we navigate being a lesbian while staying true to ourselves, avoiding the traps of societal expectations and the pressure of labels?

Because, honestly, it can be exhausting.

What does being a lesbian even mean? How do we untangle our truths from the rules others create?

This book explores lesbian identity through personal stories, historical reflections, and contemporary research. It's written for anyone who has ever questioned whether they are "lesbian enough," has felt the weight of community expectations, or wants to understand themselves better.

Together, let us challenge assumptions, question "rules," and redefine what it means to be a lesbian in today's world.

Let us seek to answer one central question:

"Lesbian, who are you?"

INTRODUCTION: *Breaking the Silence*

The first time I questioned my identity as a lesbian, I was in a Facebook group for lesbians. A poster had just finished sharing a post about her previous relationships with men. A popular member of the group said that she'd never dated men, and the heart reactions couldn't come fast enough.

"So you're a gold star?" the poster asked, dropping the heart eyes behind her question.

I felt my stomach tighten. The term has always made me uncomfortable, as it creates an artificial hierarchy within our community based on past experiences. But before I could comment, she continued:

"That's amazing. You're so lucky you never had to go through that phase."

That phase. As if the journeys of other women were somehow less valid, less real, less worthy of respect. In that moment, I realized how deeply these judgments run within our community, and how desperately we need to address them.

This book was born from conversations like these—moments where labels, judgments, and unspoken rules threaten to overshadow our shared humanity. It's written for every woman who has ever questioned whether she's "lesbian enough," who has felt the weight of community expectations, or who simply wants to understand herself better.

But let me be clear: this isn't just another coming-out story, though coming out is certainly part of many of our journeys. Instead, this is an exploration of what happens after—how we navigate our identities, relationships, and communities in a world that often tries to define us before we can define ourselves.

Throughout these pages, we'll examine the complexities of lesbian identity through multiple lenses: personal stories, historical context, contemporary research, and cultural analysis. We'll challenge assumptions, question "rules," and work toward a more inclusive understanding of what it means to be a lesbian in today's world.

You'll find personal narratives woven with research, practical exercises alongside theoretical frameworks, and always, always, an emphasis on individual truth. Because if there's one thing I've learned in my years of being part of this community, it's that there's no single "right" way to be a lesbian.

This book is both a challenge and an invitation: a challenge to examine our own biases and assumptions, and an invitation to explore our identities with curiosity rather than judgment. Whether you're newly out, questioning, or have been part of the community for decades, I hope you'll find something here that resonates with your experience.

Or provoke thought.

So let's begin this journey together, asking ourselves and each other: "Lesbian, who are you?"

CHAPTER ONE: *The Basics of Identity*

The Weight of Words

Words have power. They can lift us up or tear us down, validate our experiences or erase them entirely. In the lesbian community, few words carry more weight than "lesbian" itself.

For some, it's a badge of honor, a clear declaration of who they are and whom they love. For others, it's complicated by years of societal stigma, internal struggle, or community gatekeeping. And for many, it's both: a source of pride and complexity, joy and challenge.

As any new member of the community will tell you, there are hurdles and hoops to jump through to be thought of and accepted as a lesbian.

And I say "new" because much of the judgment stems from outdated ways of thinking—ways that fail to evolve with the diversity and complexity of human experiences.

For instance, if a woman has ever slept with a man, some still argue she's not a lesbian but either bisexual or just "curious." Similarly, if a woman has never been intimate with another woman, she's often labeled as untrustworthy or unsure of her identity.

Let's start with the basic definition: a lesbian is a woman who is emotionally, romantically, and/or sexually attracted to other women. Simple enough, right?

But within this seemingly straightforward definition lie countless questions: What defines a woman? How do we account for gender fluidity? What about past relationships with men? What role does physical intimacy play in defining lesbian identity?

These aren't just academic questions; they affect real people's lives, relationships, and sense of belonging. Take Maya's story:

"I knew I was attracted to women from a young age, but I dated men throughout college because that's what was expected in my culture. When I finally came out and started dating women, some people in the lesbian community treated me like I was somehow tainted. One woman even told me I was 'basically straight' because I'd been with men before. It took years for me to feel secure in my identity, to understand that my past doesn't invalidate my present."

Maya's experience isn't unique.

I went through the same experience in that group, and to make matters worse, I had married a man and had two kids.

Many women face similar judgment, both from outside and within the lesbian community. This gatekeeping often stems from internalized homophobia, fear, or a misguided attempt to protect the community's boundaries. But in trying to define who's "in" and who's "out," we often cause harm to the very people who need community support the most.

Where is the empathy? The acceptance?

As we continue to read, we will see some labels within the community elevate certain experiences while demeaning others. A woman who has only been with women might be called a "gold star lesbian," seen as "pure" or "ideal," while others are questioned or dismissed.

The judgment. The invalidation. The constant need to prove or explain yourself.

These judgments stem from fear, insecurity, or past trauma. But instead of projecting those feelings outward, it's time we reflect inwardly. Trust yourself, take time to get to know others, and approach relationships from a place of curiosity rather than judgment.

Who gives anyone the right to question or determine another person's sexuality?

At the end of the day, being a lesbian isn't about fitting into someone else's definition. It's about being authentic to who you are—past, present, and future.

Here's the truth:

A lesbian is a woman, regardless of her past, race, culture, or experience, who is romantically and emotionally involved with another woman. That's it.

The Emotional and Psychological Impact of Gatekeeping

Gatekeeping doesn't just hurt in the moment—it leaves a mark. The psychological effects of constantly having to "prove" one's identity can cause long-term self-esteem issues. How many times does a woman question her place in the community because others assert who she is, or isn't? The subtle erosion of confidence can lead to a sense of not being "enough," a feeling that can haunt women for years. It also impacts how we trust others and form connections within the community. We may end up hiding parts of ourselves for fear of judgment, leading to isolation.

The emotional toll can be profound—especially when the people who should be embracing us are the ones contributing to the pressure. The fear of exclusion and rejection can drive us to conform to rigid identities, even if they don't feel authentic. The longer this happens, the more we risk losing touch with our true selves.

Nicola K. Lopez is a Jamaican-born author who writes with clarity, edge, and intention. Her book *Lesbian: Who Are You?* confronts silence and brings real stories into the light. She also wrote *When The Strong Get Tired*, a collection focused on the truths caregivers rarely speak aloud. Nicola's work challenges assumptions and invites readers to think more boldly about identity and humanity. More at NikkiLopezWrites.com.

Embrace Your Roots and Let Them Fuel Your Strength
by Richa Chadha

PART ONE: *Power of Purpose & Possibility*

Lesson 1: Embrace Your Roots and Let Them Fuel Your Strength

One of the most powerful ways to leverage your strengths is to embrace where you come from— the values, lessons, and experiences that shaped you. Understanding and appreciating your roots allows you to tap into a well of resilience, perseverance, and inner strength that can fuel your journey forward. This chapter takes you through my journey and how the circumstances and values I inherited from my family became the foundation on which I've built my life and career.

A Legacy of Strength: My Mother's Story

It's often said that children absorb more from what their parents do than from what they say. I was born to a 20-year-old woman with big dreams and an indomitable spirit. My mom, a vibrant and determined young woman, became a mother to me when she herself was barely an adult. She had dreams—so many of them, but more importantly, she had the resilience to face challenges.

My mom is the second eldest of seven siblings, and from a young age, she stood out. My grandmother often described her as both "the toughest and easiest to manage," a paradox that baffled me when I was younger. I asked my grandmother to explain. She told me, "Your mom always knew what she wanted and stood firm in her beliefs. But she was also deeply empathetic, always putting others before herself."

Watching my mom, I learned that being strong doesn't mean being harsh or unyielding. It means having the courage to pursue what you believe in while remaining compassionate and understanding toward others.

One summer evening, our dining table became a courtroom. The issue? My school tuition was due, and my father, always cautious with money, felt it might be better to shift me to a less expensive school. I sat quietly, worried about losing my friends and the progress I had made. But my mother? She was ready to fight for me, and she did it with her signature blend of strength and grace.

"Education is non-negotiable," she said firmly, her voice calm but resolute. "If we need to cut back elsewhere, we will, but Richa deserves the best we can provide."

My father argued back, pointing to the rising costs and the uncertainty of our finances. My mom didn't waver. She calmly laid out the importance of consistency in my education and the sacrifices we could make to make it work. But then, as the conversation softened, she leaned in closer and said with genuine warmth, "I know you want what's best for her, too. Let's find a way to make it happen together."

Her assertiveness wasn't aggressive, and her empathy wasn't weakness. It was a perfect balance—a reminder that strength is most powerful when tempered with understanding. In the end, my father agreed, and I stayed in school.

That night, I saw firsthand how courage and compassion could coexist, how a firm belief doesn't need to crush others to stand tall. It's a lesson that has stayed with me ever since, shaping how I approach challenges in my own life.

My mom's strength didn't come without sacrifice, though. Before she married my dad, she had dreams of pursuing a diploma in music. Music was her passion, and she had the talent to go far. But after marriage, those dreams were put on hold. She devoted herself to our family, sacrificing her own ambitions for the sake of her children. This is something I admire, but also wish she hadn't done. While her selflessness was admirable, I often think about what might have been if she had pursued her dreams alongside raising us.

Growing up, I never saw my mom back down from anything she believed in. She was always the first to stand up for what was right, whether it was advocating for our education or ensuring that our household ran smoothly. She instilled in me the same values—to be strong, to never quit, and to always stand firm in the face of adversity. But from her sacrifice, I also learned an important lesson: while it's crucial to support and care for others, you must never lose sight of your own dreams.

My Father: The Strength in Vulnerability

My dad's strength was of a different kind. While my mom taught us discipline and perseverance, my dad taught us the importance of emotions—how to recognize them, how to express them, and how to use them to connect with others. He was the emotional heart of our family, always there to provide comfort, support, and love.

My dad lost both of his parents before he turned 20, an experience that profoundly shaped him. Growing up without the guidance and support of his own parents made him both vulnerable and incredibly strong. He understood the value of family in a way that few others could. Having navigated life without parental support, he was determined to be there for us in every way possible.

While my mom's approach was more structured and disciplined, my dad's parenting style was rooted in love and compassion. He showed us that vulnerability wasn't something to be feared—it was a strength. He encouraged us to be authentic, to express our emotions, and to never shy away from being ourselves. For me, this was an invaluable lesson. In a world that often views vulnerability as a weakness, my dad taught me that it's one of the greatest strengths a person can have. One memory that perfectly captures my dad's compassionate parenting style happened during my school years. I had just lost a big debate competition that I had poured my heart into, and I felt utterly crushed. As I sat in my room, overwhelmed with tears, my dad quietly walked in, sat beside me, and said, "It's okay to feel this way. You gave it your all, and that matters more than any trophy."

He didn't rush to offer advice or brush off my feelings. Instead, he simply listened as I poured out my disappointment, frustration, and self-doubt. When I had finished, he gently said, "Courage doesn't always get recognized right away, but it's always there, building you into something stronger. Standing up there and giving it your all—that was courage."

That moment stayed with me. My dad showed me that vulnerability isn't a weakness but a pathway to growth. He taught me that embracing my emotions and being authentic, even in failure, is where true strength lies. It's a lesson that has shaped not just how I face challenges, but also how I connect with others.

My dad was the balance to my mom's firmness. If I ever felt overwhelmed by the discipline of life, my dad was there to remind me to slow down, to take care of my heart, and to always lead with kindness. His vulnerability and emotional intelligence gave me the tools to navigate relationships, both personal and professional, with empathy and understanding.

Growing Up in a Traditional Joint Family

When I was born, my parents lived in a large ancestral house located in the heart of the city, shared with my paternal uncles, aunts, and cousins. It was a traditional joint family, common in our culture, where multiple generations lived under one roof. Growing up in such an environment had its advantages—there was always a sense of community and support—but it also had its challenges.

The town we lived in had a somewhat orthodox mindset. Men were expected to be the breadwinners, while women were responsible for running the household and raising the children. My dad and his siblings, having lost their parents at a young age, were thrust into survival mode early in life. This meant that they had to prioritize work over education to ensure that their families were provided for.

Many of my cousins followed this path as well. The boys in the family were expected to help with the family businesses, while the girls were taught domestic skills like cooking and sewing. Higher education wasn't always a priority. My fate might have been the same had it not been for my mom's determination to give me the best education possible.

My mom wasn't willing to settle for the local government school, where most of the children in our family studied. She had her sights set on one of the best schools in the city—a prestigious Catholic institution known for its high academic standards. Getting admitted was no easy feat. In fact, it was a significant financial strain, and my parents faced resistance from within the family.

When I was old enough to understand, Dad would often sit me down on the veranda and tell me stories about my childhood, moments I was too young to remember but that shaped who I became. One evening, as the sun dipped low and the sky turned a soft orange, he began one of his favorite tales about me.

Richa Chadha is a leadership and executive coach, mentor, writer, and founder of *Coachampion*, a coaching venture based in the Bay Area. She helps people, teams, and leaders turn challenges into purposeful pivots. Richa holds an MBA and a Master's in Organizational Dynamics from the University of Pennsylvania. Her work blends psychology, storytelling, and leadership, and she writes about purpose, courage, and human transformation. Connect with her on LinkedIn or join her coaching community on Instagram.

HIDDEN: Under my Rice
by Rita Turner

PROLOGUE

Some embrace death. Others fight, grappling to pull light into the black hole death leaves in its wake. Me? I ran from it all the way to China.

The day my husband died, the bright yellow daisies outside my kitchen window seemed to wilt before my eyes. It had been seventeen months and a life's battle lost to cancer when my husband lay dying on the sterile, white sheets of his bed. My face stained with tears, I drew in a heavy breath and nodded to my son. His eyes questioned. A moment of hesitation… then with a trembling hand, he twisted the black knob on the oxygen tank. Its final hiss trailed off into the quietude of death.

It has been one year since that day in spring when the last dry breath of death settled into Paul's frail bones. Days don't race by like they used to. They stretch out long and taut like cowhide, and the nights are pierced with whimpers of loneliness as I lie in bed caressing the cold, unruffled man side that once radiated with warmth. I can barely face the mornings, not even over a strong cup of coffee. Another day… another week–they are all the same. I walk out the door and drive to school. This morning, when I reach my car, a butterfly rests on the door handle. But I swish it away without a thought.

At my mother's funeral, I released a box of monarch butterflies that flew up into the air into a majestic swarm, but one fluttered down and landed on my sister's outstretched finger while I read the poem I wrote about my mother's life like the metamorphosis of a butterfly. The lone butterfly didn't seem like a coincidence, but something aethereal, deeply spiritual, as if my mother's soul had morphed into that butterfly. And there she was on my sister's finger, watching her own funeral. My mother was always a grandstander, and oh, how that butterfly shone in the morning light. Since then, I say hello to butterflies as if I'm greeting my own mother. But lately, in my emptiness, butterflies go unnoticed, and my passion for teaching flickers like a dimming candle.

Forty years I've been teaching, each year with the impetus to make a difference in a child's life. But soon, when I retire, that purpose will vanish, and the pencil marks of those dedicated years will be erased from the annals of my long career as though they never existed. I'll give away my prized books and projects– the life-size skeleton, my sugar cube missions and starched balloon planets. I'll close my classroom door behind me and walk away. And the next year, a new teacher, perhaps young and zealous, will print her name on my whiteboard and another cycle begins. Life goes on like this.

But where am I in this strange new place of my own life? Only two years from retirement, and here I am alone, facing my lost dreams. What am I going to do with the rest of my life without my soulmate?

"Why me! Why now!" I cry out to God.

As a child, I learned to talk to God when I knelt by my bedside to say my prayers and when that bully Max Carlson chased me up the hill, I prayed. And as a young bride, I whispered prayers of thanks when two white doves flew into my atrium and nested on the rubber tree plant, bringing me joy in the depth of sorrow after yet another baby lost to miscarriage. And after the devastating effects of carbon monoxide poisoning from a faulty heater, I prayed for healing, and again after the removal of a life-threatening tumor growing inside my spine. God was present during those valleys of my life. Surely, he hears me now?

I decide to turn in early after my emotional outburst in hope of escaping night's blanket of loneliness. I set my alarm for 6:00 a.m. on my wake-up to music radio station. In the depth of night, I startle awake to a loud voice blaring out into the darkness ... "Teach English in China and earn your master's degree..."

Untangling myself from a web of covers, I stumble across the dark room just as the voice trails off into a crackle. I whack the radio hard with my fist to hear more, but only static fills the air. Strange? I've never heard this on my morning radio station and at 3:00 in the morning? I wander back to bed and drift off to sleep to the words, *teach English in China* droning on in my mind.

It's been a week since that mysterious broadcast to teach in China, and still, those words plague me. While I eat supper in silence, they chatter loudly in my mind. And when I awaken from a night's sleep, they march boldly through my morning thoughts. I can no longer stand the annoyance and reach for the phone to call the radio station.

"No. I'm sorry." The secretary comes back to the phone. "No one knows anything about the advertisement you speak of on our radio station. Would you like a list of our sponsors?"

I spend the next few days chasing down leads, and after endless email searches for that elusive program in China, a nearby university pops me a response: *We offer a Master's program in China.* I can't seem to click the keys fast enough as my fingers fumble across the keyboard to answer back. Within the week, I manage to secure an interview with the dean of Asian studies at Concordia University Irvine– surprisingly, only blocks away from where I live.

"Tell me, how did you hear of our pilot study?" Dr. Timmons looks up from my resume during the interview.

"An announcement over the radio at 3:00 in the morning," I hesitate... "But I haven't heard it since."

He turns his gaze to the Director of Overseas Studies. "Richard, did you place an advertisement on the radio?"

"No. I don't know who would have placed a radio ad. We don't have the budget for it."

That very day I signed up for the year's program to teach English in China. Like my mother's butterfly, it feels surreal as if something divine, perhaps inevitable, is about to happen. Who placed the ad and why it aired only once as a voice in the night, never to be heard again, is an unsolved mystery. It's a closed book, but a new chapter is about to open in my own life's story. China is to become my destiny.

JUST A BOARD

Humidity drips from pores of the sky as the temperature soars above a hundred at the Hong Kong airport. "Why did I come here?" I grumble, peeling my sweat-soaked blouse away from my skin, but I know the answer to that.

Overweight and rubber bands for arm muscles, I tug at my 70-pound suitcase, inching it forward only a few feet. At this rate, I'm sure to be the last one to board our charter bus to Shenzhen. With one last determined heave, I drag my luggage across the parking lot all the way to the bus. Once inside, I grope my way down the dimly lit aisle to a saved window seat next to Marie.

Marie is my closest friend from our summer classes at the university, where we studied in preparation for teaching in China. We share a kindred bond, for we both grew up on the high plains of New Mexico and are the oldest students in this master's program.

It's quiet in the bus, and most are sleeping. Even Marie is passed out, her black-rimmed glasses tipped sideways; her straight, black hair draped over her sweater. I peer out into the Chinese night. It seems like a crazy dream... me, 8,000 miles on the other side of the world.

The bus pulls out of the station and passes through several customs checks on our way out of Hong Kong into the night streets of Shenzhen. Sealed off from Hong Kong and the rest of mainland China by entrance gates and customs checks, Shenzhen is a hub for foreign trade, a virtual haven for English tutors. Once a small fishing village, it has grown to be China's first economic zone and one of the fastest developing cities in the world, with over 12 million people.

Our first teaching assignment will be at the International English Camp in the surrounding jungles of Bao'an, the poorest of Shenzhen's six districts. As the moon disappears into the jungle, I drift in and out of sleep to the rhythmic bumps of the bus over rugged roads. Suddenly, it jolts to a stop, and I jar awake!

I press my face against the window and peer out through the gleaming headlights. A massive iron gate whines open into a military-like compound encircled by a high, chain-link fence crowned with barbed wire. Did we just enter prison grounds?

Rita Turner's works invite readers to find hope, courage, and meaning in unlikely places. Her year of teaching in Shenzhen, China, where her memoir unfolds, deepened Rita's belief in the power of resilience and cross-cultural connection. Now residing in Denver, Colorado, Rita primarily writes inspirational short stories and children's literature, with *Swing High Sally* currently in progress. Her inspirational stories are published in *Guideposts, Angels,* and *Mysterious Ways* Magazines. RitaMarieTurner. com.

Joy
by Susan Eriksson

My red-headed cow and my red-headed uncle once appeared in a dream, swimming together in a large body of water, from left to right, my uncle on the far side, both with their heads above the lightly rippled water surface. There must have been a light breeze.

Decades later, I related this dream at a friend's dinner party. Telling our dreams around the table, an English professor told me I was ridiculous. To be honest, she said my dream was ridiculous. Our host Bonnie, a poet, said, "It's Susan's dream. You can't tell her it's ridiculous." Some people say dreams are like films, and my critic that night was a professor of film.

Another decade later, diving down a rabbit hole into the internet on a lonely Sunday morning, I came across a poem — my Uncle Louis and my cow, Blossom, immortalized in a poem written by my old friend, Bonnie.

Happiness *by Katherine Soniat*

That evening, she painted her nails metallic rose,
placed the opal on her finger, and walked

down the block to a party in the moss garden.
A friend held her hand, getting involved

with the milky luminescence of the ring.
Before long, he was telling her how his uncle

loved to float down the river with a favorite cow.
And indeed that bovine figure was a fabled swimmer.

The river had a bluish tint and swirled slowly
beneath the trees. The cow with a hoop in its nose

swam on a rope near his uncle. This uncle, who had
lived alone his whole life, always spoke of the cow.

By some accounts, both could be seen as flying.

I hadn't talked to Bonnie, aka Katherine Soniat, for a few years — she had moved to North Carolina and I to Colorado and Singapore. What was it about my dream that had embedded this image in her mind to eventually show up in a poem? And it was my dream, my uncle, and my cow after all!

Blossom was rather unique among pure-bred Jerseys. Her eyes lacked a normal Jerseys rim of kohl– her hair a light red with none of the black hairs shadowing most Jerseys dainty, buff bodies.

White Dove was my first heifer, and my brother's calf was Running Bear, both named from a 1959 pop song. I was not a very good trainer that first year of showing cattle. I think my father was embarrassed by the white ribbon White Dove and I accepted before walking off the show ring.

Princess, my second cow, was better behaved, or I was just a better trainer, practicing walking backward with her halter held high in the months before the cattle shows. Washing, braiding, and fluffing her tail and then donning crisp white clothes right before entering the show ring was more up my alley.

Jerseys are small cows, and I could push this leg and that to set all four directly under her body for the judges' inspection. Princess walked off with a purple ribbon at the County Fair and with the Grand Champion purple rosette at the Broadhead Fair. If you drive through Broadhead, Kentucky, today, the boarded-up storefronts on Main Street and derelict fairgrounds reflect the current economic situation in much of rural Kentucky. But in the mid-20th century, that fair was quite a thing. Alas, in the State Fair arena, Princess stood on my foot and leaned into me, her body cock-eyed as the judges walked by — another white ribbon, the ribbon of shame.

And then came Blossom. I don't remember the ribbons, although by not-remembering, she probably got a blue. I loved that cow. She stood in the stanchion that Princess had occupied and that Sue had occupied before that, a stanchion at the end of the row of cows next to the calf pens and closest to the radio that, in winter, continually played music to lull the cows into giving up their milk. Even as a teenager engrossed in piano lessons and boys, I stopped by to see Blossom.

Uncle Louis, probably known in the 1950s as a confirmed bachelor, smoked Camels, grew dahlias, and made me laugh. A veteran of the WWII South Pacific Theater, he lived alone in the house where he grew up. Louis Jr, as we called him, taught art at the high school at one point, but he was largely unemployed. A bit of the 'crazy uncle who comes to Thanksgiving Dinner,' he always spoke of his dog, and the last time I saw him, he chastised me for not asking about him. I was an adult when he died, and only then did I hear he had frequented the legendary bar at 224 East Main St. in Lexington, known from 1939 as a place of discretion.

Bonnie tells me she doesn't know what time had lapsed between hearing the dream and writing the poem, but that she revised it many times and chose the garden and the ring as the setting for the poem.

"Blue topaz," she said.

"No, an opal," I replied. I had read the poem more recently than she had. To me, opal was more perfect than blue topaz for the poem, more interesting, and far more mysterious. Opals are fragile, solid, but not crystalline. Tiny spheres of silica in lines and layers break white light into opal's rainbow. Any old topaz can be irradiated by humans to turn blue, but opals' colors are magic.

And I could be that girl in the poem, putting an opal on my finger — an Australian open brought home by my husband from a two-month field season studying the sedimentary geology of Mount Isa, Queensland, Australia. At some point, no doubt,

I went to a party with that opal on my hand. But I never painted my nails a rose tint. I would have gone for peach.

About that ring in Blossom's nose. Putting a ring in a bovine nose is for bulls. Jersey bulls have a reputation for being mean. I don't know if it is true, but if I were confined to a stinky, dark, small room and fed grass through a hole in the wall two times a day, I would be an angry bull. So when you trot me out to hump a cow – my only purpose in life – with people watching and a potentially unwilling cow, I'd need a ring in my nose, too. But not sweet, Jersey dairy cows. Cows wear halters when you walk them. *Happiness* has some poetic license, which, as a former dairy princess, I find amusing. As a scientist, I find lack of precision annoying.

Did you know there is no word for a single 'bovine' creature? The plural is cattle, but a single animal is a calf, heifer, steer, cow, or bull.

I don't make a habit of trying to remember dreams, no waking from a deep sleep and describing my dream with the pen and paper next to my bed. I don't analyze them in the morning light. I always read to my young daughter before bedtime, perhaps inducing fanciful dreaming.

> *Hey, Diddle, Diddle*
> *The cat and the fiddle*
> *The cow jumped over the moon.*

Cows can do amazing things. A girl in Germany wanted a horse. Her parents said no, so the girl taught her cow to take her on its back to gallop across the meadow. They even learned to jump.

If a cow can jump over the moon and a girl can ride a jumping cow, of course, Blossom the fabled swimmer in *Happiness* belonged alongside my uncle. The uncle had great powers, and the cow could actually fly with him. Nothing ridiculous, when you think about it.

Perhaps the dream was actually a film, and I woke up before I saw other people and animals swimming along after my uncle and cow.

Perhaps Louis Jr. painted her portrait, and in the last year of his life, perhaps Blossom and her last calf lived with him and his dog in the shed behind the dairy barn.

Perhaps this is how myths are made.

[Happiness was published in Image Magazine, Issue 67, reprinted by permission of the author.]

Susan Eriksson, a geoscience researcher, museum curator, and educator, has worked in industry, academia, and the non-profit sector. Her writing draws on her early life on a Kentucky farm and decades of interacting with rocks and people on several continents. Her book-in-progress explores the many ways we can see the Earth. She regularly shares her thoughts in the newsletter EarthToSusan.substack.com and at SusanEriksson.com. *Joy*, a departure from her Earthly obsession, is her first published essay.

ADULT
FICTION

Category Winner:
The Pearl Farmers
by Stacey Gordon

Late in the morning on the day that altered her family's fortune forever, six-year-old Penny Louise Lockshire slouched back in her lukewarm bath, sulking. She glanced up at the ceiling and gasped.

The sight of a tightrope of cotton-candy cobwebs stretching between ceiling globe lights normally wouldn't cause her to jolt upright in panic, momentarily forgetting her campaign of self-pity. Her mother was no domestic goddess and never aspired to be. A distinguished, bloomy rind ordinarily coated the surfaces of the Lockshire home, filling Penny with a fizz of comfortable affection. No one expected perfection in this house. Far from it.

But for the past six weeks, Mama had purged, scrubbed, and dust-busted to get ready for this weekend, because Daddy insisted these two days had to go flawlessly. A weird energy had taken over the family: her goofball father had grown stern, her dreamy mother galvanized, her older sisters too preoccupied to pick on Penny, until she actually missed the teasing.

The stakes, apparently, were high. And now here hung this forgotten cobweb. Imperfection: unacceptable. What if this ruined everything?

Then Penny remembered: she didn't feel particularly charitable toward her parents this morning. In spite of the stunning blue skies and soul-warming sunshine outside, her parents insisted on keeping her locked inside this indoor prison all weekend. Like the house itself, she was expected to stay pristine and sanitary. Quiet, well-behaved. To somehow appease a crowd of strangers Penny had no desire to know.

Resuming her pouting, she slid back down to chin-level and stared glumly at her belly rising out of the graying bath water like a dormant volcano. Downstairs the screen door slammed and slammed. Since late morning she'd watched out the upstairs window as cars drove up their long driveway and parked on their broad front lawn in rows. People climbed out of them and up the lawn in small groups, carrying green and yellow Tupperware with the same name written in black marker on the lids: LOCKSHIRE.

On any other day, she would have rolled out of bed and run down to the lake before bothering to eat breakfast. Her skin prickled with longing for the silky water and the cold mud and satisfying scratch of shells against her feet.

But her daddy had laid down his ultimatum a few nights ago. "Stay out of the lake this weekend, Penny Louise, or I'll tan your hide."

She'd laughed at him when he said it. He sounded so silly. Her parents, normally too distracted to enforce discipline, let Penny roam the woods and waters surrounding their property at will. If she'd ever heard talk of tanning hides, it had been on TV.

But her father James's face remained stern.

"I'm not kidding around, young lady. Don't try me."

Penny, who would try anything, hadn't decided yet how she planned to respond to this challenge.

***

The preparations for the Lockshire family reunion had begun during Penny's final weeks of first grade. One balmy afternoon, she'd disembarked from the school bus to see black smoke rising from the back of their house.

Like most country people, the Lockshires burned their trash, but usually only on Sunday evenings. Curious, Penny climbed the driveway and rounded the corner of the house. She found her mother, Kate, in the back, wearing a pink apron and stacking a decade's worth of *Life* magazines into a milk crate.

"Collage, Mama?" It was a reasonable guess. Ordinarily, a stack of magazines in Kate's hands meant she was about to embark on a spontaneous new project she'd dreamed up that day.

"Not this time, baby."

Penny dropped her book bag and sat on the back stoop. She watched as her mama fed the ravenous fire in the steel drum with the raw materials of her creativity—pile after pile of fabric, paper scraps, newspapers, catalogs, ribbons, and buttons.

Over the next few days, the rooms of the Lockshire house grew airier. Penny became newly aware of the crisp lines of tables and the actual colors of walls. Meanwhile, their normally cheerful mother grew increasingly somber.

"Why is Mama burning all her stuff?" she asked her sister Helen before bed one night. Normally, Penny hated the nights her officious older sister handled her bedtime routine. She tucked Penny in with taut sheets that left her breathless and only agreed to read baby books because they were short.

But she knew thirteen-year-old Helen to be wise. Plus, her older sister had been preparing for the family reunion by studying the Lockshire family tree—*Jeannie-ology*, she called it, as if Barbara Eden could fold her arms and poof up devotion to people Penny had never met.

Helen, in the middle of reading *Brown Bear, Brown Bear, What Do You See*, sighed at the interruption.

"The Lockshires are coming," Helen said.

"But we're the Lockshires." Penny knew this to be true.

"We're not the only Lockshires, peabrain. Daddy has a big family, full of lots of cousins, aunts, and uncles. And his sister Sue is coming from California."

"But why does that mean Mama has to get rid of all her stuff?" Helen's explanation didn't justify the erasure of their mother from the landscape of their home.

Helen snapped the board book closed. Relieved, Penny plucked *Brown Bear* out of her sister's hand and set it aside.

"Okay, so you know how Daddy's great-grandfather built this house when he moved to Tennessee a hundred years ago?"

"Yes."

"Well, even though Daddy inherited the house from his dad, the house kind of belongs to the whole family. Mama and Daddy are sort of its caretakers, of the house and the family business. And Daddy wants his family to see that he's taking good care of it all."

"But…"

"Mama's collection was starting to get out of control. It was time to clean it out anyway. But I think they didn't want to give Daddy's family another reason to not like Mama."

Penny stared at her sister. Who wouldn't love their mother?

"You need to help Mama, too. Don't be wild. The three of us, you and Anna and I, need to be perfect children this weekend. Otherwise, Daddy's family is going to think she's a bad mom."

"She's not a bad mom! She's the best mom!"

"So do what she tells you and promise not to be a peabrain."

"I promise." Penny meant it at the time.

***

The bathroom door opened, and Kate burst into the room. "You've been in the tub too long, Penny. Let me dry you off."

"I'm not a *baby*, Mama."

Kate spread the towel open like a flag. "Out."

She climbed out, letting her mother wrap her in the towel and rub her short hair dry with the end of it. Kate yanked a starched, gingham dress off a hanger on the back of the door. Penny recognized the dress as one formerly belonging to her sister Anna, who'd fought wearing it as hard as Penny was about to.

"I'm not putting that on," Penny informed her mother.

"Yes, you are."

"I am *not*."

"Penny," her mama said in a low, even voice. "This weekend is very important for your father. We are all giving up something to make it a success."

She remembered her promise to Helen, but Penny couldn't find it in herself to be good. She locked eyes with her mother. For good measure, she stomped her foot.

When she was much older, Penny would remember this moment and understand why Kate softened. Her mother's only hope of getting through the weekend with any dignity was to keep peace with her daughters.

"Fine. Put on shorts. Go outside and play with your cousin Aaron from California. But do not go near that lake. Your daddy will tan your hide."

Penny couldn't believe her luck. In a brief moment of gratitude, she pointed up at the ceiling. "You missed some cobwebs, Mama. If you want to knock them down before someone sees."

Her mother blinked twice at the ceiling, then flashed a mischievous smile and winked at her daughter.

"Go."

Penny was out the door before her mother could change her mind, slipping through the crowd of family members as deftly as a fish escaping a net. No one could hold onto her now.

***

She found her cousin Aaron sitting under the sycamore tree. She'd expected someone tan and blond, like the California people she saw on TV, maybe with a surfboard under his arm. Instead, he was pale, skinny, and freckled, with spiky red-brown hair.

"I'm Penny," she told him. "We're cousins."

He turned his indifferent gaze onto her.

She tried again. "Let's play."

"It's too hot. And this place is boring. I've never even heard of Ferry's Landing, Tennessee, before this weekend. It's poor and ugly here. What is there to do, anyway?"

They could hide in the woods, or make necklaces out of white clover, or catch frogs in jars and dress them in doll clothes.

Stacey Gordon is an author of book club fiction, mysteries, and short stories. A former journalist, she started her career reporting on the jewelry industry and now works in experience design for tech companies. Her short fiction has appeared in *The Avalon Literary Review*, *Waxing & Waning*, and *The Capra Review*. *The Pearl Farmers*, her debut novel, will be published by She Writes Press in November 2026. She lives in Alameda, California, with her family. StaceyGordonAuthor.com

Half-Life Horizon
by Bruce Rettig

half-life
> 1) the time required for one-half the atoms of a given amount of a radioactive substance to disintegrate.
> 2) a brief period during which something flourishes before dying out.

PART ONE

"We need the possibility of escape as surely as we need hope."
~ Edward Abbey, *Desert Solitaire*

"The optimist thinks this is the best of all possible worlds. The pessimist fears it
is true."
~ J. Robert Oppenheimer

CHAPTER ONE
Las Vegas, Nevada. January 26, 1951, 11:23 pm.
Muted light reflected across bottoms of cocktail glasses stacked upside down along the back bar. Up front, bottles of well liquor—rum, vodka, gin, brandy, whiskey, scotch, bourbon, and tequila—filled a speed rack. Above them, two shot glasses, one metal, one glass, sat on the drip edge. Onions, olives, cherries, and freshly cut lemons rested within garnish holders. A line of twelve ashtrays stretched lengthwise across the bar top, glasses stuffed with plastic toothpicks shaped as miniature swords between each one. Residual odors of spilled alcohol, cigarette and cigar smoke, cologne and perfume remained as permanent residents, their essence seeped deep into the contours of the casino barroom.

Conrad Cooper took a box of napkins out of a cupboard, pulled out a handful, and placed them on the bar top, the Fremont Hotel & Casino Bar logo side up. He then set a beer glass sideways on top of the stack, applied pressure, and twisted it to fan the napkins into a helix. After setting the swirled stack at the end of the bar, he pulled another handful of napkins out of the box and continued the process, a comforting task before the night shift began.

He turned to the mirror behind the bar, his reflection partially hidden by shelves of liquor bottles. His eyes appeared as though they belonged to someone else, piercing brown gatekeepers concealing wartime apparitions and heinous mementos. If he kept moving, he could stay one step ahead before the flashbacks completely devoured his soul. He leaned on thoughts of walking out of the casino bar in a matter of hours, driving out of town, the Vegas skyline growing smaller in the rearview mirror. A trek across the desert to an undetermined destination catalyzed an unyielding desire—

possibilities to satisfy a yearning for something, anything, that might replace a seemingly unfillable void.

In that same desert, stationed within a secluded area approximately sixty-five miles northwest of the city, and eight miles south of designated ground zero, atomic test technicians scratched notes on clipboards hanging on a cinder block wall constructed a few days prior. The building included a control room, administrative office, first-aid station, and shower for personnel decontamination. Two photography stations, one to the southeast and the other to the northeast, would capture images less than two miles from ground zero. All these outposts resided within a 680-square-mile region known as the Nevada Test Site, or NTS.

The technician's notes contained several sheets verifying test factors: weather conditions, including wind direction, and an outline of potential risks that could impact results. All equipment, with calibrations double-checked, continued to function properly as a radio operator validated the proper operation of communication systems. He made a final callout to the surrounding outposts and confirmed that the test area remained clear of unauthorized personnel, vehicles, and aircraft.

The NTS Test Commander walked out of the control center and peered at the glow of Las Vegas through binoculars, then turned west to a waning gibbous moon. A shooting star arced across the sky and a nearby coyote cried out. He focused on its shadowy image as it scrambled down a shale bluff lit by moonlight and followed the animal's path as it wound its way through patches of sagebrush covering the desert floor. A verse ran through his head: *they shall be given over to the power of the sword; they shall be a portion for jackals.*

Everything in its place; a sense of order. Five hours, thirty-seven minutes to detonation.

***

Conrad considered eighty-sixing the two barflies after one knocked over a cocktail glass for the third time, rejecting that decision after looking at his wristwatch—4:31 am. Only thirty minutes left. He pushed his anxiety into the chasm that harnessed his volatile emotions so many times before.

"Maybe you've had enough for one night." Conrad turned the glass upright and soaked up the spill with a bar rag, relieved that it might be the last time he mopped up someone else's mess for a while.

"Sorry, can't hear you. Music's too loud." The fortyish, bottle blonde shot Conrad a wink. Across the crowd, the band struck up *Atomic Baby*, a newly written tune by blues musician Amos Milburn.

"Night's 'bout gone—morning's 'round the bend," slurred the other woman, who wore a white dress with black polka dots. She lifted a pack of Lucky Strikes from her purse, pulled one out, then held it to a mouth framed by cherry red lipstick.

Conrad gently freed the cigarette from her fingers and spun it around so the filter pointed toward her mouth. He picked up an open match book, bent a match over, and deftly lit it one-handed. The woman took a quick drag, then exhaled a thin column of smoke that joined the lingering haze above the bar.

A ringing bell and metallic clanking of coins cascading into a hopper signaled a winner at the slot machine near the end of the bar. "Not a jackpot, but better than nothin'," a man yelled to his friends over the boisterous crowd.

Revelers danced and sang along with every song the band struck, sloppier and more incoherent as the party gained momentum with each cocktail served. The specialty drink remained a crowd favorite—the *Atomic Cocktail*, a near-toxic concoction of vodka, brandy, cognac, sherry, and champagne over ice, shaken well, then poured into an oversized champagne glass and topped off with an orange wedge on the rim. A bartender at the Desert Inn's Sky Room had created the recipe, and as with every hot Las Vegas gimmick, its popularity traveled fast and most every bar in town served the new drink. The absorption of this alcoholic mixture into the bloodstream, combined with the influx of nicotine from smoking, amplified a dizzying brain bombardment.

As Conrad filled a row of glasses with ice, his thoughts shifted to his first day of bartending in the smoky confines of the Fremont Hotel & Casino Bar. It had provided a refuge, a safe place where he could regroup.

Conrad had hit the road a couple of months after returning to the States. Having completed his fourteen months of service in Korea and receiving an honorable discharge, he tried to carve out a life back home in upstate New York. Although surrounded by family and friends, nothing felt the same as before he left. His Father was the only one who could remotely relate to the battlefield experiences. He had fought in World War II, serving as a medic, patching up soldiers to get them back on the field, or sent home in pieces. Conrad couldn't tell him about the events that occurred during the horrific days at a bridge called No Gun Ri, shameful of the atrocities he witnessed. Conrad carried that weight alone.

The world he once knew had kept moving, and people's lives went on, but he had been pushed several steps backward. His life remained out of sync with everyone else's, so he traveled west to Nevada, an open doorway—an opportunity to breathe and do whatever the hell he wanted without people asking a lot of questions. He could find a place where no one knew him, and an opportunity to start over. He hadn't expected meeting a cocktail waitress named Gina, who was also running from, or to something.

"C'mon, sailor, how 'bout a couple more drinks down here?" Bottle Blonde begged.

"As I said earlier—I was Army, not Navy. You're welcome to sit and enjoy a cigarette and listen to the music, but I've cleaned up enough spills for one shift."

Conrad thought it ironic that he'd been of legal age to kill men, but not old enough to serve alcohol until returning home and turning twenty-one. For a while, the mundane bar work had extinguished what he referred to as the "flashes"—lightning shots of sounds and images bombarding his mind like shrapnel pelting an open battlefield; ingrained memories of gunfire, explosions, blood, pain, soldiers shouting, and women and children screaming.

Ultimately, the bartending routine merely served as a temporary elixir for a chronic condition, and Vegas merely a temporary stop. The flashes had returned. Scar tissue fades but never disappears. *Keep moving*, Conrad told himself, *keep one step ahead of them.* His old sergeant's voice reaffirmed the thought: *If you don't keep moving, you're a sitting duck…*

The house band finished their rendition of "I've Got You Under My Skin," and the master of ceremonies walked to the middle of the stage and grabbed a microphone from its stand. He wore a loose red-plaid jacket, dark pleated tweed pants, and white shoes with gold tassels.

"Ladies and gentlemen, may I have your attention?"

Bruce Rettig is the author of the multi-award-winning Refraction: *An Arctic Memoir*, inspired by his time as a merchant marine in Prudhoe Bay, Alaska. His new novel, *Half-Life Horizon*, set during the 1950s atomic testing era in Nevada, is a stark, poetic tale of survival, identity, and the cost of freedom. He also works with the American Indigenous Tourism Association, supporting Native storytelling. Rettig lives and writes in the high Sierra. More about his work can be found at BruceRettig.com.

Sorry Cakes

by Catherine Forster

CHAPTER ONE: *Day One, 1953*

The second hand twitched, as if unsure of its task, before striking. The sound was a silky "bong," neither harsh at the beginning nor dull at the end.

Judyth listened to the comforting timbre, welcoming the calm after Easter's chaos when harried parents and a rowdy gang of grandchildren and nieces and nephews took over the house. It had taken a week to prepare, and she'd looked forward to their arrival, but once they charged in, she fled to the kitchen, her refuge, where she busied herself, shutting out the uproar.

She bent down and placed her ear on the clock's surface. "You're sounding a bit labored." Wrapping a dust cloth around her fingernail, she tackled the grime pinned in the clock's crevices. "It's time Ed gave you a good cleaning."

The purchase of a *Seth Thomas* was Ed's decision. Judyth recalled his rejection of fancier models, not because of the price, but because of their tone. The clock was their first purchase as newlyweds, and he was determined to find one that complemented her nature. "One that purred," he'd said. The absurdity of it made her laugh. When had she ever *purred*?

Keeping time with the clock, she rubbed the glass dome shielding its face. While she poked and buffed, Judyth recalled how her son had made a point of avoiding her during Easter. "Tony could have come into the kitchen for a short chat," she said, waving the dust rag in the air. "I had no time to follow him around. Meals needed preparing." Following her outburst, Cookie made one of his own. An audible pop echoed from the Spaniel's jaw. His teeth and tongue were exposed, and his mouth remained open as if stuck in slow motion, then snapped shut. The dog stood upright with one leg forward.

"I'm not speaking to you. Stay put," she said, recalling how Tony sat between Ed and Karen during dinner, distancing himself from Judyth as if eager to avoid her.

Judyth picked up the mantel clock's neighbor, a glass paperweight. She held the paperweight at eye level and peered inside. It was sea-blue, like a Caribbean postcard and a prized possession. Deep inside, countless flowers bloomed. As a child, she imagined fairies playing hide-and-seek among the flowers, inviting her to join them. Looking closer, she discovered something odd on the surface.

"Sticky fingers," she said, her lips curdling downward. She put the globe under her nose and sniffed. "Marshmallow. Must have been Peeps."

At the mention of Peeps, the dog jumped to its feet. Despite repeated reprimands, the children kept feeding him the candy, which he licked dry before burying it. "Cookie, stay— I've no time to play." The dog whined and lay back down.

"The culprits had help," she whispered, noting that those old enough to reach the globe knew better. An adult must have assisted. And it wasn't Ed. He would have wiped it clean before putting it back. Judyth retrieved a damp cloth and removed the sticky obscenity. When pristine, she placed the cool surface against her cheek, and for reasons she could not explain, imagined her firstborns, a girl and a boy, playing among the flowers inside the globe. A leaf became a makeshift slide and the boy lunged for it, rushing past his older sister. But she wasn't outmaneuvered, and the two descended together.

Annoyed with herself, Judyth set the paperweight down, handling it rougher than she intended. As a rule, Judyth avoided thinking about them—the boy was with her for eleven months and the girl for just two weeks. She snapped the dust rag against the fireplace as if attempting to purge the unwelcome thoughts. She had no patience for morose contemplation. In her mind, only weak simpletons carried on about things they could not change.

The doorbell rang.

Her eyes shot to the door, as did Cookie's. The bell rang again, then two more times.

"Lord, who could that be?" she grumbled. It was Wednesday, dusting day. Every day had its purpose, but Wednesday was her favorite. Dusting required little effort and allowed her to reacquaint herself with the many treasures she had collected through the years. She did not like being disturbed by unwelcome thoughts or people knocking at her door.

"For God's sake, stop pushing the bell."

No one dropped by, except for Bible peddlers who came calling all too often, mistaking country folk for the lonely, or hoping for a friendlier reception than townies put out. Judyth didn't resent the gospellers who came to her door. They were doing God's work, but she didn't need their preaching. She heard enough of that on Sunday mornings.

"Oh fudge, not now," she said, loud enough to be heard through the door. A warning. Stern-faced and ready for a showdown, she opened the door.

"Hello," Tony said, holding a suitcase. His six-year-old daughter stood by his side, her face hidden in the folds of his jacket.

Surprised to see them, Judyth stood rigid. Her eyes narrowed as she stared at her son and the suitcase. "Tony?"

Judyth searched for their car, expecting Karen to be watching from the passenger seat. She located the Studebaker, a clunker, but Karen wasn't there. Guilt swelled, souring Judyth's stomach. She had not visited since the twins were born, yet they had come over for Easter. Judyth had volunteered to help, but her offer was rejected, not outright, but Karen had made it clear that they could do without her. Karen's mother was coming to stay.

"I wasn't expecting you," Judyth said, recalling the evening she met Tony's mother-in-law, how Helen had fawned over him, and how he'd responded in kind. Tony clearly envied Karen's upbringing and would have traded mothers had he the opportunity. "I wish you'd called first."

"I need a favor."

"Aren't you coming in?"

"I have to get back to work."

She waited for him to explain. When he wasn't forthcoming, she became agitated. Her gaze jumped from him to her granddaughter. "What's this about?"

"I need you to take Janet for a while. We can barely keep up with the twins. Janet has stopped speaking. Not a word since Easter. We don't know why, and yes, we've tried to figure it out. Karen is overwrought. Exhausted. I'd like to do more, but I have to work. I don't like asking—"

"What's wrong with her?"

"Karen?"

"No. Janet."

Judyth glanced at Janet, expecting a reaction, but the child did not flinch upon hearing her name.

"Karen thinks she's acting out. Maybe jealous of the twins." He looked down at his daughter and said, "I agree. And they're not going anywhere, so you best get used to it." When the child refused to look at him, Tony rolled his eyes. "Whatever we've tried has made no difference … only made matters worse."

"What do you expect me to do?"

"Since Janet is close to Dad, Karen thought bringing her here might help."

"Your dad is supposed to fix her? That's ridiculous. Besides, how can she be a bother if she's silent? Take her home and give it time. She'll come around."

"Karen's at her wits' end."

"What about Helen? I thought she was going to help out?"

"She went home yesterday. Said the same thing as you—we should wait it out."

"Good advice."

"Mom … I'm not asking."

"Excuse me?"

Tony wiped his forehead and squeezed his eyes shut. After a moment, he opened them and glared at her. "Dammit, Mom. I don't want to fight. You owe me. A second chance—and she's your granddaughter."

"Owe you?"

He bent down and whispered in the child's ear, "You be good. Grandma is strict, but she loves you. I'll be back soon. I love you. Mommy does too."

Janet didn't respond, not even a nod.

Judyth pretended she didn't hear him. He shoved the suitcase inside the door, then turned around and left. She watched his stiff body descend the steps and march across the lawn to his car. The child watched until the car was no longer visible. Judyth looked down at her granddaughter. She was wearing a school uniform that needed washing. Her hair had not been combed. Her socks didn't match, and her hands were dirty.

"Best come inside," Judyth said, imagining a brown ring around the child's collar. "You know what to touch and what not to touch."

The child stared at her feet. She didn't move, not even a cursory nod. Judyth, the dog, and the child remained silent and still for an uncomfortable period. Judyth wished Ed was home and had been here to confront Tony. He'd know what to do. *Let him fix her.*

"Grandpa will be home soon."

She nudged the child inside. "First things first. Those hands need washing."

Janet lifted her chin just a little and stared straight ahead.

Catherine Forster is a writer, visual artist, filmmaker, and independent curator based in Olympia, WA. Her artwork and films have exhibited widely in the US and abroad. Literary awards and publications include the Pacific Northwest Writers Association's Women's Fiction finalist, plus short story and poetry publications in various journals. *Chasing Tarzan*, a memoir, was published in 2022. She is an avid kayaker, hiker, wife, and mother of three dynamite kids.

Bitch Coyote
by Jen Eve Thorn

PROLOGUE: *In The Canyon*
JULY
ANDREA

"What matters, Suz, isn't that you have the trail mix. What matters is how you got it."

Nora shoves Suz to the ground, reaching for the shovel as Suz rolls over and crawls away from her. Nuts, raisins, and candy-coated chocolates lay scattered in her path. Suz doesn't make it far before Nora leaps onto her back, still wielding the shovel and using her free hand to press Suz's face into the dirt. I think we'd all agree, well, maybe not Suz, how she got the trail mix *is* what matters most. The slide back to our before selves might happen just like that.

Gill can't resist joining in, leaning over and spitting in Suz's matted hair. I notice for the first time that Suz has never really been blonde at all; her roots have come in. How strange to think I've never known this part of her; maybe the trail mix is just the tip of the iceberg? What is most egregious, somehow, is the punctuation of the little candies in the dirt, each round and shining candy, a color out of place.

"Have you been sneaking home?" Nora hisses into Suz's ear. "Or did Damon leave food out for you?"

It would be impossible for Suz to answer with her face in the dirt and Nora's knee grinding into her spine. Gill gets down on her hands and knees next to them, intoxicated and sort of rabid with the justice she can smell coming. Suz begins pissing herself, a trail of urine making its way through the dirt from beneath her.

"Did he feed you like a pet, Suz? Did Damon leave a little bowl out for you, like his fucking house cat? Did he lure you home?"

Suz struggles, one arm reaching behind her at a painful angle, trying to gain traction somewhere on Nora's body, the other arm pinned beneath her. But even if Suz can get her nails in, Nora won't let go. I look to Jules beside me; she's stunned like the rest of us. I wonder, not for the first time, if we have arrived at wild; are we just now crossing the line? Then Nora brings the shovel down on Suz's skull, and it makes a sound, a specific sound. It's a gross sound and my stomach caves with the impact, but it's also exhilarating. This feels better than safe.

I can see my yard in the distance. If we all looked up, we would see our fences and potted palms from this vantage point where we exist now, in the canyon behind our homes. If our families are looking down, they can probably see only our colored hats, like candies in the brush. Perhaps they're wondering if today is the day we'll finally choose to come home.

PART ONE: *Before The Canyon*
FEBRUARY
ANDREA

The heat inside the locked car holds me like a mother, pressing in from all sides. Pets and children die in cars like this, so could I. They'd find a sort of jerky of me, browned and twisted in the driver's seat. I *could* start the car, get the air going, roll a window down. Instead, I adjust the rear-view mirror to see my reflection. Hair is stuck to my face, clothes are filthy, hands are caked.

I hadn't anticipated nine miles; the trail guide said seven. I'd failed to account for the distance from the parking area to the trailhead. Best laid plans and all that. I curl my toes against the grit in my boots; I'll carry it all the way home because I'm not opening the car door to shake it out. I peel off my shirt and use it to wipe my face and sticky hands before stuffing it into a plastic bag with my untouched lunch. In my sports bra, my back sticks to the faux-leather upholstery and sweat travels the rolls of middle age, gathering in the creases.

One thing at a time, that's how I'm supposed to be doing things now. First, start the car, then drive home, then shower; I don't need to think beyond that. I refocus the rear-view mirror. The small brown sign with the white arrow, indicating the direction one might *eventually* find the trailhead, appears again in the reflection. I start the car and the white arrow shrinks in the distance as I return home.

***

"How was it?"

The drive was a blip. I was in the car, then here on the couch, showered with a cup of tea steeping, staring out the big windows overlooking the canyon behind our home. Greg was in his home office when I came in, in video meetings, words like *metrics* and *deliverables* occasionally floating out to catch my ear.

"Quiet, " I say.

"I bet, it must have been nice to go in the middle of a weekday," Greg approaches from behind the couch, resting his hands on my shoulders.

I know he means it kindly, Greg means everything kindly, which makes it worse. *Must be nice in the middle of the day, out traipsing around the trail.* He begins rubbing my shoulders. I feel so aware of his touch, aware he can probably feel my tension building. I consider telling him to stop, then consider telling him more than that.

"You could go down and hike in our canyon," he says, abandoning the shoulder rub and walking into the kitchen. "You don't have to drive somewhere else to hike," he adds, searching the cupboard for a snack.

"But there's no trail down there," I counter, "and snakes."

Greg opens a bag of chips.

"I think there's a bag that's already open," I call out.

"I don't like those ones as much," Greg crunches.

I listen to him crunching. I love Greg. I love him, AND he chews loudly. I can hear him across our open-plan living room/dining room/kitchen. This is why there should be walls between rooms, for chewing sounds.

I look out over the canyon, which drops off dramatically on the other side of our pool. Just out of sight, over the canyon's edge, a fence separates us from the urban wild, but from here it appears there's no barrier. It looks desolate, but not barren, a blanket of brush occasionally broken by palm or cactus. What's that paddle cactus called? Can a person even walk down there?

Greg continues through crunching. "I think there are probably as many snakes down there as where you just were."

"What if something bit me while I was down there, Greg?"

"Then I would see you foaming at the mouth and I'd come save you," he says, returning the now-opened bag to the cupboard, next to the other already opened bag of chips. He must have eaten three chips in total. His self-control is maddening.

I don't think you foam at the mouth from a snake bite. I think that's rabies. Didn't he see *Old Yeller*? Greg crosses through the space that *should* be three rooms divided by walls, leans over, and kisses me on the head. "I'm glad you're relaxing," he says, before returning to his office.

Relaxing. Before taking a leave of absence, relaxing was what I did in between working. What is relaxing now, without the bookends of work? I should get up and get that shirt out of the car. I should put it in the trash. I should wipe my boots off. I stay on the couch. I must be *relaxing.* I don't feel it though; my whole body hurts. I finish my water diligently, at least I'll be better hydrated now that I'm relaxed.

Hiking was on the list my therapist encouraged me to make, the list of what I'd like to spend time doing while on leave. Hiking came right after baking bread. That bread shit isn't going to happen. Liking fresh bread doesn't mean I'll become someone who bakes it.

I return to the big windows that look out over our pool, a bright turquoise "free form" shape which is really just a kidney, a beautiful kidney set on the edge of Myrtle Canyon, which certainly must have had a different name at one time. What happened to the canyon's original name? It probably went the way of all indigenous names developers feared were too complicated to pronounce. Myrtle is a grandmother's name.

A line of stucco houses snakes along the rim of Myrtle Canyon, every other house the same model in a different shade, pools sparkling and palms potted. Maybe I should hate the repetition or be embarrassed by it, but I think it's soothing.

Surely my neighbors would see me wandering down there, in my yellow baseball cap, picking my way through flesh-snagging cactus. What if I were lying on the ground? Would someone spot a body in the brush? *Do* you foam at the mouth if a snake bites you?

Jen Eve Thorn is a writer, director, and public speaker. *Bitch Coyote* is her debut novel. She's honored to be a finalist for the 2025 San Francisco Writers Conference Contest and a nominee for Best Microfiction of the Year 2025. Thorn's work has appeared in *The Los Angeles Review, Flash Fiction Magazine,* and *Raw Lit Magazine.* She's one of the founders of MOXIE Theatre and lives in San Diego with her husband and teenagers. JenEveThorn.com

Babe in the Hearth
by Kate Spires

CHAPTER ONE
Age 12

The trailer park was actually pretty fucking cool if you weren't a total dick about it. Samson kept all the bulbs in the string lights lit, always, and my propagation skills had won me an award when I was ten. Now, every "porch" had little green guys that lived 'cause of me and my mustard watering can of a prize. I didn't love having friends over, but I loved living like a rain stick when the storms hit our tin roof, and my mother let me have the bedroom while she took the couch. I used to think that was decent and now I know she'd've slept under the axle if it meant I was warm. If it meant I laughed louder than anyone in "Songs River," the community of people who'd dipped from the system and then wouldn't shut up about it.

"Beautiful, beautiful girl," she used to call me before my tits entered the scene.

Then, "Smarty Pants McGee," when she found the tampons I bought without telling her, 'cause sometimes she could be too much about all that.

Three weeks shy of thirteen, I turned her and I into costume glitter.

I came home from Aline's place where I'd been turning all my shirts into crop tops. Didn't say much when I went to the fridge 'cause the hair dryer was on, so I waited until that engine roar settled down.

"You'll never guess what someone called me," I said when it did.

She'd promised to get the good pudding, the swirl kind, so I didn't see her face when she rounded the corner. I was too busy looking for it, sliding over her orange juice. *Her* orange juice. The special kind she drank at night. The bottle I kept pretending I didn't know was mostly tequila.

"Uh... Chickadee McGee... Kennedy."

"Laugh Out Loud. No." The swirls were behind *my* orange juice. No booze, just a splash of grenadine she'd brought home from work. "Beautiful, beautiful girl. Isn't that crazy?"

She whipped the fridge door so far back it broke off its hinges.

We didn't have fridge door money. We barely had swirl money.

"Who the fuck said that to you?"

"Indy."

A not-so-old man who'd never meant any harm but never really meant much of anything. Just sorta lived halfway out his window, shirts always ripped on the thorny latch.

"When?"

"Just now."

"Stay here, Beatrix," she said.

"Stay here?" She'd never told me that, not once. 'Cause there was never anything out there that could get me.

"Stay here."

Her liner was thick only on one eye and it made her look like she was blinking. If she'd slammed our front door any harder, we'd've lost two doors that day, but the ol' tin one stayed on and rattled against itself, trying to decide whether to slip off or hold tight.

From the kitchen window, to the back one, to the bathroom, to my room, I kept track of her. She was too young to be ratty but just old enough to be cartoony, hair in rollers and bouncing as she walked. In one slipper and one tennis shoe. I smiled a little as she passed Mrs. Morrow's place. Then Samson's. Then Grady's.

Then she was at Indy's.

When I was a kid, I thought he was skinny from cigarettes. My mom told me that was a thing, but looking back, there were track marks on his wrists and noise that blurred his eyes. None of his clothes ever fit, ever, and I'd thought that was just how he liked to dress.

She formed a fist usually used for sourdough and beat hard on his door.

Waited about a half breath.

Beat hard on his door again. Trying to smash through the metal as best she could.

Then she shouted so loud she was practically in the room with me, so she must've been the sound of fury on his doorstep.

"Get the fuck out here!"

Her voice rattled all of Songs, and for some reason I ducked down for a second before popping back up.

"Indy, open the fucking door!"

He did, but the door handle dragged his torso out and he stumbled. She shoved his shoulder to keep him up.

I couldn't hear anything after that. She leaned so close to him, spoke so quiet only he could hear her. 'Cause she thought 'beautiful, beautiful' might catch all our vans on fire. Spread wild and free until I no longer had a name besides that one. The one she gave me before knowing I'd live up to it.

They both looked at me too long, then she shoved him back inside, and when I thought she would finally come home, she sank to the steps and cried. Proper, straight-up. I caught Samson's eyes from his kitchen window and he frowned to say, *What on Earth?*

I shrugged to say *This, I think, is about me, but I don't have anything to do with it.*

Any other day, I would have walked over there before her shoulders even started shaking, but she'd told me to stay, so I stayed. Honestly, not because she'd said anything but because it seemed important. Because Indy had looked at me like I'd be dead tomorrow, and he was the one who'd killed me.

My mother pressed her hand to her mouth to try and keep silent. Across the way, while she hung out some laundry, Mrs. Morrow shouted to her, "'Kay, Sasha?"

"Yeah," she said, voice opening only enough to create sound. "Yeah, I'm cool."

So god damn cool.

She eased up and off the steps, pushing herself forward with her left hand.

She was still wiping her eyes when she got back and said, "he's not gonna call you that again. So, don't you think about it."

"I don't get why it's a problem."

Her face was the same she made when I brought fabric in from the dumpster to use for dresses. "Yes, you do."

Meaning dawned on me bright and early.

"Mom, c'mon, that's not... that's not here yet."

"They don't wait on girls like you," she said, still not looking at me. "Sometimes it's sixteen."

Lord. Of course it was that, and where I'd had a feeling she was in one of those moods, that just confirmed it. With a huff I was getting good at using, I dropped onto the couch and shoved my feet into the cracks between the cushions.

"No one gets assigned at sixteen, Mom."

I'd thrown the first punch. *Shit.*

"*Taken*, Trix," she said. "*Taken* at sixteen."

She grabbed my face, thumb and middle fingers in each dimple, and jerked my head toward the living room mirror.

"And yes, they do."

The next morning, all my new crop tops were restored to their original length with fabric from her own closet. The next afternoon, she stole the make-up kit I'd been given in drama class, "You can have this back for tech week."

As if any of any of that could've prevented what happened. My mother, three eyeshadows and cherry red lipstick, waging war on inevitability.

Three weeks later, it came in the mail.

A manila envelope. No return address. Just an American flag stamp.

My mother had burned her own, so I'd never seen one in person.

***

Dear Beatrix Sarett,

Community, Continuity, and You

That's right, *you*! We are the Bureau of Civic Continuity, often better known as The Hearth Program. This pamphlet offers a brief look at what's ahead. Some of it may already sound familiar, shared by a parent, teacher, or friend, but we believe it's important to be clear. That's why you're receiving this personalized guide.

Requirements and Practices

Girls are eligible for placement, colloquially known as assignment, as early as sixteen. This may sound so far away, but guess what, it'll be here before you know it!

*Statistically, 95% of young women are placed between 18-21 years old.

Boys and girls are matched by proximity, intelligence, and genetic testing. You're going to love him, we promise, and you may even know him already. Either way, you'll meet on your big day!

Three children are required within the first five years of marriage. This serves multiple purposes:

1. *Preserves our national population*
2. *Demonstrates marital fitness and civic unity*
3. *Promotes genetic diversity for a resilient future*

Have questions?

All licensed teachers and guidance counselors are trained on our rules and regulations, and they are there to help you through this transitionary time in your life. So, do not hesitate! That's what they're there for.

Never forget, you're not alone.

This country was made for you

And you were made for it.

The future is closer than you think. Let's build it together!

Kate Spires, born and bred in Texas, is a literary writer with a brain that treats pop culture like psalms and functions like IMDb. A 4th-generation Austinite, she obtained her MFA in screenwriting from Loyola Marymount University and currently works at the historic Paramount Theatre in her hometown. Connect with her on Instagram @katieb10193.

The Man Tree
by Kayla Ogden

CHAPTER ONE

Ardern, New Verda

2085

The world had heard about our man tree. Photos of it had slipped onto the real internet, but the images were deemed AI-generated. By then, New Verda was already known to be a forsaken place, but an organic tree made of fused body parts? Such a grotesque thing, such a magical thing—it was beyond serious consideration.

I blame the Verda Crown Order. We all do. They are the fools who created cerino sheep.

The first time I learned of the cerino sheep was three years ago, in November of 2085. The memory of the day is as clear and bright as the day itself had been. I was at the kitchen table, going over our accounts on my laptop with Frank, my AI, in his nest. My brother, Luca, came in and dropped his gloves into the basket by the door. Dad followed, stooping to untie his boots. Their faces were rosy. They had been helping the new lambs feed on colostrum, which always left the men sweet.

"What is there, Chloe?" Dad asked me.

"Check the pan and I'll take a plate," I said, blinking and scrolling my eyes along my screen.

Luca lifted the lid from the pan as Dad grabbed the plates.

"Yum, what's on this?" Luca asked, sweeping his sweat-curled brown hair out of his eyes.

"Just eggs and sausage. Some fresh herbs from the box," I said. "Rosemary and thyme."

"You take good care of us," Dad said, scooping up the scramble as Luca bent beside me to peck my cheek.

I grunted but blushed just the same.

There was a knock at the door, and Frank's face shifted from a blank metal sheet to a screen which showed a woman standing on the step. I picked him up and placed him on my shoulder, where his feet spread into claws which gently clung to me.

I walked through the house, adjusting my plaid shirt sleeves and collar, tucking my hair behind my ears.

"Yvonne MacAbee," Frank whispered, "From Verda Crown Agricultural Innovations."

"Never heard of her," I said. "Or Agricultural Innovations."

"Yvonne MacAbee is a sales rep. Low seniority. Unmarried. Anemic. I have a high iron recipe to bolster her. Would you like to see it?"

"No. Why haven't I heard about Agricultural Innovations?"

"Agricultural Innovations was first documented publicly in a press release approximately 6 months ago. It's relatively new," he said.

"What isn't?"

"Is that rhetorical, ma'am?"

"Yes, now be quiet," I said as I slipped on my loafers and opened the door.

Miss MacAbee was dressed in a bright white dress shirt and gray skirt – too nice for a farm visit – but she had paired it with rubber boots, which I found endearing.

"Hi," she said. "I'm Yvonne." She held out her hand and I shook it. "Are you Chloe Tussok?"

"The one and only."

She looked from my face to Frank, and then back at me. She laughed softly. "Forgive me, but is that a Frankaphonic? I've never seen one in person."

I grinned. "Do the thing, Frank."

At this, my robot jutted the metal cube that stood for his hips from side to side, bobbed his head, and lifted his arm in a lassoing motion. "Giddyup, giddyup," he said. He had a few dumb tricks like that.

Yvonne covered her mouth with her hands. Her green eyes lit up.

"Now rest," I said. Frank settled back to form.

"That was adorable. I didn't know those things still existed."

I nodded. "He's the best."

I agreed to follow Yvonne down our front path to where she parked her shining pickup and trailer. I stepped back and aside, expecting the sheep to jump out when she opened the doors. But the sheep stood eerily still, side by side. They opened their eyes in tandem, stared at me for a beat, and then closed them again.

"You can inspect them."

I climbed into the trailer and crouched before one of the docile things. Its nostrils were narrower than those of any sheep I had seen before. It emitted a soft snore with each breath. As I drew my hand away, the wool lifted, following my skin.

"You getting this?" I said quietly to Frank, who beeped once in a covert "yes".

"You no longer need to shear," she said. "Give them this pill when you're ready, and they will shed their fur in three days. They should live through five or six cycles. When they expire, they must be buried deep — not eaten or burned." The Crown would replace the sheep, as they did not have sex organs to reproduce.

"What are those?" Luca asked. He and Dad were standing in the grass now beside Yvonne at the base of the trailer.

"These are the new Cerino Sheep. You're getting a sneak peek," Yvonne said.

Dad and Luca's chests inflated. Flattery would get you everywhere with those two. I bristled. The Verda Crown Order sent merely one person and two sheep to my farm for this pitch? What a shoddy show for what was once the penultimate merino wool-producing farm in the nation. Production had shrunk since my mother left. As her eldest child, I knew it was my fault. But our brand, Tussock Wool, still held weight.

Yvonne held her hand above her eyes like a visor against the brightness of midday. She said, "I'd love to tell you all about them. Can we go inside? Or somewhere shaded?"

Yvonne didn't bother shutting the trailer doors. From the passenger side of her truck, she grabbed a rolling suitcase before leading us along the path to our own house.

In our sitting room, she opened her suitcase and placed a microscope on our coffee table. She slipped a slide under the lens and gestured for me to look. I saw that each fiber of cerino wool was a hollow tube. The sight of it gave me the heebie-jeebies.

"Would you like to compare it with the merino wool?"

"I know what merino looks like," I said. "It doesn't look like that."

"Don't be rude, Chloe." Dad said from where he sat on the sofa next to Luca.

Would I like to be a part of New Verda's textile revolution? No, thank you, and excuse me, but I would not. Dad and Luca weren't happy that I refused. They thought the fashion cycle idea was genius. Cerino wool couldn't be dyed. When it was introduced, everyone in New Verda would wear white. Then suddenly, you would spot a beautiful person wearing a blue cerino pullover. An announcement would be made — we've developed blue sheep! Folks would jump to add blue to their wardrobes. Then yellow, and so on and so forth.

"How do you know you will be able to produce blue sheep?" I asked.

"Because we already have."

I felt so old then, though I was only 22.

As it turned out, the Verda Crown Order didn't need me or my farm. A few months after the rep's visit, we received a survey about cerino wool men's underwear in our weekly bundle.

The surveys and bundles were popular at that time. We weren't required to fill out any survey, but a gift would arrive in the following week's bundle for each form we completed. Being an island nation, certain products were missing from the grocery stores or pharmacies at times.

But the Order would come through with these items as bundle gifts: a bar of soap, a bag of coffee, a pair of AA batteries.

We received a survey which only asked the men of the household to state their underwear size. The gift would be a package of 5 cerino wool boxer briefs for each man. Why not socks? Why not dish rags? Why did it have to be so personal?

The briefs were well received. They were exceptionally stain-resistant, softer than wool, breathable and cool.

They looked sexy when Perry wore them. My neighbor since childhood tried the underwear on and danced around his room. Our relationship was finally evolving, something I had dreamt of since puberty. The underwear looked uncanny, like glossy white paint on his skin. I peeled them off him. I called him a traitor — but I was on my knees, smiling up at him when I said it.

Better not to think of that now, as I pack. Or ever, really. If crying were productive, it would have done something for me by now.

The second annual Vigil Day is almost here and I don't know what to expect. Last year was too soon. But I know I paid for Perry's name, along with my father and brother's names, to be put on the memorial "forevermore". I hope the names are etched deeply in stone. My plan is to travel to Lorde City and touch the edges, the valleys, feel the solemnity and purposefulness with which they were carved. What else can I do to ease the pain?

Kayla Ogden is a Canadian fiction writer based in San Mateo, California. She is currently seeking representation for her debut novel, *Pillow Forts Down*, which explores the dark edges of adolescence in 1980s and 2000s Vancouver. She co-hosts the writing-craft podcast *Write Your Heart Out*, sharing practical tools, spicy conversations, and plenty of laughter. You can find her on Instagram @kaylaogdenwrites and @ writeyourheartoutpod.

Shadowed by Death
by Mary Adler

CHAPTER ONE
Northern California. 1944

The silence woke her. She pictured the lighthouse beacon pushing against the mist, warning hospital ships of one last hazard between them and home. She was in the Presidio, but she heard no voices, no laughter, no slap of rifle stocks against palms. Only silence, then footsteps scuffling the winter-dead leaves.

Squealing hinges, a jerk, and her shrouded body thudded to the ground. Her head bounced as he dragged her through the night, over rocks and branches, sticks and stones. She opened her mouth to scream she was still alive, he didn't have to do this.

And then her uncle's voice came to her over years and miles, over the edge that separates the living and the dead. She heard him tell again how the bear had gripped his skull. How he had stilled his breathing and gone limp and hung from its snout forever, his weight heavy against the points of its teeth, his eyes closed against its burning saliva. Then the bear tossed him to the ground, circled him, nudged him with a paw. Once, then again. He didn't move, just held his breath and prayed.

And then it went away, crashing through the woods. When he stopped trembling, he limped back to the cabin and poured half a bottle of precious vodka over his head. The rest he drank.

Or so he said as he held her under her chin and looked into her eyes. Bears are much stronger than we are, so if a bear ever gets you, go limp little one. If you do not struggle, if it thinks you are dead, it will lose interest, and maybe—he raised a finger and touched her nose—just maybe, it will let you go. She had smiled and said there were no bears in the city. Ach—he cocked his scarred head—you never know.

She could not fight this human bear, but she could pretend to be dead, as dead as the family she now knew had perished in spite of her sacrifice. She clenched her teeth and swallowed her pain. All the years of her loneliness, she had believed she would embrace them again one day, breathe the air they breathed, feel her face cupped in her father's hands. The bear had promised.

Now she promised to make a dagger of her sorrow and kill him for what he had done.

He yanked her feet and dragged her from side to side. The shroud muffled her cry and sheltered her from the mournful wind rattling the eucalyptus leaves. One great shove and the shroud unfurled, spinning her to the creek below. It was dark and peaceful, private and deep. A good place to dump a body in the December night.

CHAPTER TWO

There was a body. Finally. I pushed toward the Bayshore Highway, slowed by the fog that had rolled in overnight and filled the shallows in the Point Richmond hills. Only my familiarity with the road and a ghostly white fence saved my neighbor's victory garden from a devastating invasion. I turned the wipers on, then off when they scraped the windshield, then on again when the road blurred into a gray smudge. A gust of wind shredded the fog and revealed a group of children huddled in the street.

A girl waved her arms, signaling me to stop, and took a few faltering steps after me. I doubted mine was the first car she had tried to flag down and imagined her disappointment as drivers ignored her. Harley, my German Shepherd, woofed when I braked, and he had to scramble to stay on the seat. I wanted to keep driving, to get to the crime scene in the Presidio, but I made a U-turn and parked behind the group with my headlights facing oncoming traffic. If nothing else, I'd move the kids out of the street before some drowsy defense worker plowed into them.

A barrage of raindrops hit the roof. I knew from harrowing childhood experiences that the trickles of water in storm drains became rushing rivers without warning. Maybe children really did have guardian angels, and maybe sometimes they showed up as strangers who were late for work, although I suspected Harley was the one with the angelic mission, and I was merely his instrument.

The girl ran to the car as I struggled into my poncho, and surprised me when she greeted Harley by name and grabbed my free hand. He wagged as if he knew her and started to follow, but I signaled him to stay. She told me about their predicament—her word—in breathless bursts while she pulled me to the corner. "A dog ran out of the bushes and my friend's stupid cat jumped out of his arms and flew into the sewer, and now he can't get it out."

A boy lay in the street with his face pressed against the mouth of the drain. If the opening had been bigger, I'm sure he would have crawled into it. I tapped on his yellow slicker and spoke quietly, so I didn't spook the cat.

"Come on out. Let me help."

He scrambled to his feet and looked at my cane with an expression just short of insulting.

"My arms are longer than yours, son, and this calls for reach, not speed."

He looked at the cane again and said "*Okay*," but his lack of confidence in my abilities couldn't have been clearer.

"Her name's Macaroni." He looked to be about eleven years old, but the fear in his eyes made him seem younger. "The water's getting higher really fast."

I bent my good leg, half fell onto the street, and crawled to the opening. I could have asked Harley to help me maneuver, but I doubted the cat would find a canine presence reassuring. The shivering marmalade kitten clung to some flotsam, its mouth opening and closing, its cries drowned out by the water that threatened to sweep it away. I asked one of the girls to run to the fire station for help and to tell them not to use their bells or sirens. Fat chance. I doubted the firemen could operate without sound effects. In the meantime, I'd do what I could and try not to make things worse.

Usually, frightened animals know you're there to help, but the kitten may have been too young to trust that instinct. I slowly stretched my hand into the sewer until my fingertips pressed against a sodden mass of vegetation. Now it was up to the cat. I waited without moving. Barely breathed. My shoulder ached from holding the position so long, and my chest felt chilled from the wet street.

The cat touched my hand with one tentative paw, then snatched it back. I held as still as I could, and suddenly Macaroni scrambled up my arm and clung to my shoulder. I held her with one hand and scooched back so the boy could disengage her claws from my poncho. When he had secured the cat, I called Harley and used his harness and strong shoulders to help myself up. The girl who had flagged me down said, "Lieutenant Wri…," but her words were lost in the wailing of a fire truck speeding toward us, making enough noise to scare the cat right back into the sewer. She looked at me and rolled her eyes. I laughed out loud and winked at her, then Harley and I took off.

A body waited for me.

CHAPTER THREE

I made good time across the Bay Bridge to the Presidio, only to be held up at the Lombard gate. While I waited for a stalled truck to get moving, one medical bus after another materialized from the mist, passed between the stone pillars, and vanished. Men looked out the windows, some taking in every detail, some with that thousand-yard stare. Like me, they had survived the Japanese killing machine in the Pacific more or less intact and had made it home for Christmas. While some families would celebrate, others would lament how changed the men were, how bittersweet the homecomings.

I shook off my thoughts and focused on my driving, accompanied by the conflicting emotions that had plagued me since my first homicide case: regret for the victim and her family, and an unseemly exhilaration at being able to do the job I loved—a job that required someone to die violently, unwillingly.

The rain sharpened the medicinal smell of the eucalyptus trees that, however unpleasant to some, was a welcome change from the stench of war that had oppressed me on Guam.

I limped along the edge of the hill and met the man who had found the body. Technically, the man. Actually, if it hadn't been for his terrier, the woman would have lain by the creek, half-hidden in the weeds, until the earth claimed her.

Mary Adler is the author of the Oliver Wright and Harley WWII Mystery Trilogy set in Northern California. She is active in Sisters in Crime and the Short Mystery Fiction Society. She volunteers for Sonoma County Wildlife Rescue and admits to being in a co-dependent relationship with her two adopted dogs from Mexico. Visit her website at MaryAdlerWrites.com.

Overcast
by MFC Feeley

Cloud-cover diffused the dawn, smudging the cliffs, beach, and boardwalk into smears of gray. No horizon scraped sea from sky. The tide folded in low liquid sheets of graphite. Sheldon's boots dragged in the soft sand, twinging his knee until he reached the water's edge, where the surf packed the shore like wet cement. He shoved his fists deep into the pockets of his sweatshirt, the morning breeze chapped his lips. Pipers sped back and forth, dodging the surf and dipping their long beaks into the tight, bubbling holes that advertised hidden clams. Gulls, so white they looked like tears ripped open by an eraser in over-penciled paper, swirled above, ready to rob the smaller birds of their hard-earned prey.

To Sheldon's right, the shadowy mounds of the Tilt-a-Whirl and the Round-Up hugged the ocean side of the boardwalk. Behind those rose the rectangular arcades, and behind them the Giant Dipper, Northern California's last, great wooden roller coaster, scribbled across the paling sky.

Like a face recognized in the dark, Sheldon's brain filled in the image of the wharf with details that were accurate, though not yet visible through the heavy fog. The green and black algae velveting the hundred-year-old Douglas fir pilings that tourists assumed were Redwood. The rising arm of the parking gate at the base, the stretch of over-priced restaurants in the middle, and warped tackle shack at the end. The railings that girded squares cut through the planking so children and their adults could watch sea lions lounge on the cross beams below. When Sheldon was a kid, he thought the wharf looked like something a giant had constructed with telephone poles. Now the wharf looked like only herself, but everything else: driftwood, rail ties, even the boardwalk, long since smothered in concrete, resembled a would-be wharf. The Giant Dipper was her shadow, loud, twisted, and in need of psychic repair.

Under the wharf, braided tentacles of foam, ridged with copper, glistened in the early light before dissolving into the sand. Something round and smooth, something shrouded in seaweed, had washed up behind a piling.

Sheldon unhooked the hatchet from the toolbelt he wore whenever he worked on Gary's boat. He hoped he was looking at a sack of garbage and not an octopus, though that would explain the gold foam: octopi have copper-based blood. It looked more like a seal. It's sad when any creature dies, sadder still to watch innocence suffer. Sheldon could stop that. Chopping up dying, and even dead, seals defied human law but using them for bait honored the laws and life cycles of the sea.

Sheldon widened his eyes to take in more light. The shiny black thing shifted with the backwash. It could be a trash bag of rats gorging on crusts and cotton candy, but the smooth curve indicated a seal. He patted his pocket. The kitchen trash bag he kept ready had survived the last wash. He'd save the seal if he could, but, if she'd been dead too long, any partially digested fish in her guts might explode on impact with his ax head. People still talked about a whale that had washed up and exploded back in '72, three months before he was born. The saw his dad used to cut into her stunk for years.

Sheldon would go to the shed and smell it. He'd pressed his nose against the rusty blade so often that he conflated the odors of oxidized metal and fish. Now, he pulled his sweatshirt collar over his nose prophylactically, ready to stand upwind, to chop and shove the bugger into his bag.

Gripping his axe, he visualized the sailfish and sharks he'd catch with seal meat. *Or a giant octopus,* he chided himself. There'd been sightings, and his boss—his friend— Gary had booked more tours this month than at the peak of whale watching season. Like every local, Sheldon dreamed of seeing the *Ophiuchus* himself. This was the real reason he'd accepted Gary's offer of a job working the tour boats, although the idea of sharing the experience with tourists degraded it.

Ostensibly, Gary needed Sheldon's help because his back was finally giving out from all the sacks he'd taken protecting Sheldon on the football field back in high school, when the Santa Cruz Pirates almost won the state championship, before the town was ransacked by yuppies and finished off by programmers. "You owe me," Gary would joke, rubbing his lumbar spine like an old man, but everyone knew Gary was doing Sheldon a favor. Still, Sheldon often caught Gary wincing as he threw a rope or bent to tie the spring line, and with all the Octopus sightings lately, he really did need Sheldon's help taking tourists on the water. When it was really busy, Sheldon treated some of the overflow to "private cruises" in the motorized skiff. If nothing was booked, Gary let Sheldon take that same boat out fishing. Gary said two boats were one too many; the plan was for Sheldon to buy the skiff once he saved twenty thousand dollars. What he should have done, he thought again, was buy that first boat, the *Alibi*, the one Gary had acquired the night of the playoffs. It was no one's fault but his own. Gary had offered to sell Sheldon the *Alibi* for a song, but every time Sheldon got the cash together, all he could see was Hadley on the night of the accident. She had begged him to go to the ER and look at his leg. How sad she looked, relenting and climbing on board. It wouldn't have made any difference. The fracture was there already; waiting hadn't made it worse.

The haze burned through the fog and gleamed off the sand, making the space under the Wharf seem darker. Gulls began to circle and dive towards the bag. One dove, and the shape jerked as the bird landed and perched on it with outspread wings. Something pale and fleshy shone under the gull's talons. Sheldon shaded his eyes. The curves of the drowned seal resolved into a naked female hip, made rounder by the way she'd tucked her legs into her belly. Sheldon sprang forward, shouting and waving his arms. The bird took off.

She lay at the very edge of the lapping water, just under the wharf. Shifting shadows gave the impression she was moving, but when Sheldon crouched to touch her foot, it was cold. Just like Hadley, the night she drowned, the night of the playoffs, the night Gary forgot the play and left Sheldon open to the injury that ended his football career. The girl's legs kicked. Sheldon grabbed her salt-slicked calf. She went stiff, then limp. Her face lay buried in the sand. Her body and the spray of her hair were so matted with seagrass that the weeds seemed to grow out of her. The whole mess of her shimmered when light bounced off the incoming waves. Standing over her, Sheldon's shadow merged into the crisscross lines under the wharf. He fumbled his ax back into place.

The beach was at its emptiest. Past the wharf, a pair of surfers in wetsuits were catching the first waves in front of the Dream Inn. Some homeless huddled under the bandshell. Near the steps to the boardwalk, an elderly couple waved twin metal detectors across the sand. Above them, a go-getter in pink headphones and yellow Lycra jogged down the boardwalk. Back where they'd sunk the old cement ship, a teenager threw a snot green tennis ball into the surf for his golden retriever, the dog as wet and matted as the girl. If alive, the girl might resent interference. If dead, witnesses would remember Sheldon's axe. The fishermen casting lines off the end of the wharf didn't know his name, but they knew which boats he worked, and they'd recognize his old Pirate's sweatshirt with its silver Jolly Roger on the back.

But the girl might need a hospital.

Sheldon hauled her up the beach and rolled her on her back, one salmon-pink nipple poked through the seaweed. He looked away and his eyes fell on the downy mass nestled between her legs like a sea urchin. He waved up at the wharf and shouted, "911!" into the wind until one of the fishermen on the old wooden benches stood up. "Please be breathing," he whispered, peeling the sheet of wet hair off her face.

Disintegrated California mussels give the northern beaches a distinct blue-gray cast compared to the orange sands of New Jersey or the pink Caribbean, but this could not account for the mottled green of the girl's cheek. Sheldon's fingers against her lips were too raw to detect any breath. He pressed his lips to hers and sucked and blew like he remembered from Boy Scouts.

[End of Excerpt]

MFC Feeley lives in Alaska and has an MFA in fiction from the University of Alaska Fairbanks. She was a resident writer at The National Willa Cather Center, a Fellow at the Martha's Vineyard Institute of Creative Writing, and is a board member of 49 Writers. Feeley wrote a series of ten stories inspired by the Bill of Rights for Ghost Parachute and has published in *Best Micro-Fictions*, *SmokeLong*, *Jellyfish Review*, *Pulp Literature*, and others. More at MFCFeeley.com

The Black Year
by Mimi Drop

1968 was a *shvarts yor*, as my mother would say. A black year, yes.

The night my mother's memories became mine, we drove forty miles over icy roads from South Bend, Indiana, to Benton Harbor, Michigan, for an evening bat mitzvah. The girl, Rachel, was a distant relation, but we had so few, my parents labeled any connection a cousin or uncle or aunt. I had no expectations other than flirting, dancing, and cake.

Built in a former cornfield, the new synagogue hunkered down in a blank landscape as the last streaks of light poked through the bloated belly of low gray snow clouds. In the parking lot, my sister Carol strode confidently over the ice in spike heels. I swore under my breath, trying to stay upright in junior pumps with slick soles. My parents, stalwarts as always, inched over the snow in sensible rubbers.

We hung our coats on a rolling rack in a tiny room off the lobby. I hurried after Carol, who dashed to the ladies' room. Her beige wool sheath, borrowed from a college roommate, showed off her golden hair and green eyes. As she pulled out one magic wand after another and leaned into the mirror, I tried to memorize the tilt of the eyeliner, the thickness of the mascara, and the careful buildup of shiny pink lips as she transformed from natural beauty to knockout. My father and I had black hair and nearly black eyes; Carol was an anomaly. I called her a freak when I wanted to make her mad.

"Ready?" she asked.

I rolled up the waistband of my skirt to make it shorter and pulled out the lip gloss stashed in my bag. My boobs had grown to adult proportions, so I'd hid a red halter under my sweater until the dancing began. "Yeah, I guess so."

Carol took out her blue eyeshadow and smudged a little over my eyes. She took a swipe with the mascara. "That's better." It was.

We hurried to the sanctuary, the only finished room, a wood-paneled hexagon soaring to a point with stained glass in modern blocks of irregular squares. My sister gossiped in the back with the older kids, but my parents made me sit with them in the third pew. The rabbi murmured prayers in a monotonous atonal drone. Occasionally, he'd end a sentence with a high-pitched grunt so the congregation would say *amen*.

My parents had a confusing relationship with religion, and although they were fiercely Jewish, they acted like they didn't want anyone to know. I'd only seen the inside of a synagogue once or twice and was fascinated by all that had been kept from me. The blonde brick building was very modern, with cinderblock walls in the lobby and long, angular windows facing the driveway. The sanctuary itself held ancient relics: a teak wood ark punctuated with Stars of David, Torahs defended by filigree lions, and an Eternal Light, a twisted olive branch made of hammered bronze holding a single flickering flame.

My father wore his favorite fedora and a bristled tweed suit that padded his already round belly. His calloused hands clutched a battered prayer book he'd brought from home. As he recited the prayers, his eyes remained shut and his lips barely moved. I fingered the fringes on his silky tallis, braiding and unbraiding them into thirds while he swayed and murmured. When he talked to God, as he often did, he sunk into himself, transported to a different plane of existence where praying made sense.

What did he think about when he mumbled and bowed? Maybe the ancient language connected him back to his childhood in Iza. I'd heard about the tiny Czech village so many times I could describe his wooden house down to the yellow dirt floors. His family of twelve lived in three rooms, sharing beds and even shoes. The names of all his brothers and sisters lived in me like a poem I'd memorized in fifth grade: Hershel, Ezra, Dov, Ruchel, Bluma, Fruma, Leeba, Perle, and Shayna. None of them survived the war. I wasn't sure how I knew this, except he only spoke of them in the past tense. Maybe he prayed for them.

On the *bema*, the bat mitzvah, Rachel, chanted a few prayers in halting Hebrew. I hoped that signaled the end, but Rachel retired to a chair in the back as the rabbi took out his notes to begin the sermon, "Tonight, we must let go of the past."

As the rabbi went on, my mother crossed her arms over her chest. In our house, the Holocaust, the war, the past itself was not to be disentombed. This, I suspected, was why my family didn't go to synagogue, why I never attended Hebrew school. My mother didn't want me to think about what being Jewish meant. She'd given up on God, or perhaps she couldn't forgive Him. As she glared at the rabbi, a deep sadness flickered over her face, and I felt an uprush of love and anxiety. I'd never understand her life, and she couldn't possibly understand mine.

Finally, we filed into the social hall. A banner spelling *Mazel Tov* and two baskets of pink and white carnations tried to brighten the space. Looking around for anyone familiar, I caught sight of the Feldman twins, Sam and Seth. I'd met them years before at another gathering of the tribe. At sixteen, their curly hair towered above their heads, and they wore Nehru jackets made of bronze brocade right out of *The Monkees*. As they turned, their eyes glittered in the overhead light as blue as goys'.

"Hey, Balin," shouted Seth, the cuter one, though they were nearly identical.

Sam cupped a hand around his mouth. "Grace!"

I waved and grinned too broadly from the receiving line. As the crowd inched forward, I recognized Miriam, Rachel's sister, nine months older than me and already sixteen. She wore pink, too, the exact shade of my mauve skirt. Her hair absorbed the light, as black as mine.

A bald man whose head shone so brightly the lights painted a glow around his crown chuckled when he saw us together. "Look at this, two peas in a pod. I'm gonna call you…The Pinkies." He wiggled his little fingers. "Get it? The pinkies."

I exchanged a glance with Miriam in mute sympathy and kissed her powdered cheek. Her hair was sprayed into a perfect flip, and Lily of the Valley cologne surrounded her head in a sweet-smelling atmosphere. We hadn't seen each other in years, but I remembered the welcome relief of meeting someone with immigrant parents of her own. I never invited gentile friends to the house because my mother might commit some social offense like offering chopped liver or worse, asking where their parents had been born. Miriam was different. We knew each other in a minute.

Miriam flipped her hair with two fingers. "I'm glad that's over. My mother dragged us to services every week when Rachel was getting ready for the bat mitzvah. Did you have one?"

"Nope. My parents aren't into that stuff."

"It's such a bore. I flat-out refused."

Adults clamored behind me. I mouthed, *See you later*, and shuffled out of line, bumping into Seth. "Oops, hi."

His teeth formed a straight line of dazzling white, braces removed, highlighting a jaw that had already formed a mature square. Up close, he was even cuter. "Hey, are you related? I forget."

"I think she might be like my third cousin, or maybe fourth." I reached up to rub my eye and remembered the eyeshadow.

Sam arrived at his brother's elbow. "This is our first bat mitzvah." His jacket hung a little looser, and his boots had trying-too-hard heels. The twins lived in Bridgman, a tiny village of fruit farms, hay wagons, and Seventh-day Adventists, with too few Jews to support a synagogue. At the time, I didn't think about why Jews would settle in such a hostile environment. I didn't understand that for Jews, nearly every environment is hostile.

"Want to go outside?" Seth leaned over and whispered into my ear, "We have a joint." His cologne, a mix of citrus and sandalwood, made my pulse jump.

Surveying the room, I found my mother hunched over the dessert table, wrapping frosting-decorated "Rachel" mints in a paper napkin to sneak into her handbag. Her behavior around food was often embarrassing. And she freaked out in a crowd, especially a crowd of Jews, and even stuttered when she said the word "Jewish" out loud. She'd gone so far as to give us Christian names, or as Carol put it, Jew camouflage. Of course, with accents as thick as my parents', hiding was wasted effort. Turning my shoulders to block the twins' view of her, I said, "Okay, let's do it."

Mimi Drop's fiction has been published in *Flash Fiction Magazine, Bright Flash Literary Review, THAT Literary Review, The Woman in the Glass,* and *OnTheBus,* and is anthologized in last year's San Francisco Writers Foundation Anthology. Her commercial work has appeared in the *New York Times, Vogue Magazine, Harper's Bazaar,* and dozens of television commercials. She's been a finalist in the Novel Slices contest and was longlisted in the Masters Review contest. Connect with Mimi at MimiDrop.com.

Laurel and the Man of Many Hands
by Oscar King IV

Deep in Laurel's chest, something had taken root. Not metaphorically—a real seed had made her flesh its soil. Its roots tangled around her ribs; its ivy wound through her insides. Daily, she gnawed the resin seeping between her bicuspids; peeled off the sappy scabs that solidified between her breasts and across her midriff. It was a kind of eternal pregnancy—alive, but never fruiting.

This spring, she was sure it would consume her whole.

But if it did, she wouldn't have to worry about being late to work anymore.

She hurried down the street, panting. This week, she was a barista. The pay was worse than when she was a marketing consultant, but the job was about more than just money. She'd loved learning how to carve shapes into the milk foam: ferns and maple leaves, and, fitting for the season, half-bare trees like lonely sentinels.

As she ran, sap-mingled sweat began to percolate on her forehead. She could feel people's eyes slide off her, as if they sensed the offness—some gut-level aversion that the world reserved for the not-quite-human, the slowly-being-replaced. She didn't mind it anymore. But she noticed it. Always.

Though it was autumn, the morning was summerish. There were never stable seasons in Larcebrac, the Sinking City, grandest and *strangest* in all the world.

True, every city is strange in some way; like quilts, all are made of separate patterns and mismatched shapes. They have downtowns and financial districts, have kiddy parks, libraries and universities—suburbs and malls like cankers that refuse to die.

Larcebrac had all that, yes. But it had it in *quantum*. It was a quilt made not of patterns, but of ever-shifting inkblot tests. You could find anything you needed in the city, anything you imagined: fairies and gods and demons and deals, tools and sciences and colors, shades, mathematics and meanings.

She hadn't yet reached her second turn down the street when something tugged at the hem of her pants. A small pinch, just above the ankle.

She looked down to find not a child, but a single disembodied hand clinging to her pant leg. She slowed, and the hand dismounted, using three of its fingers to stand while the others, like antennae, regarded her warily, then began to point back the way she'd come. She regarded it warily right back.

Harbingers like these weren't entirely rare in Larcebrac, the Imagine Nation, but she'd learned better in her two-and-a-half decades than to follow strange appendages so easily.

But the hand was persistent. As she began again toward work, it scurried after her, hopping and jumping and scrabbling until it blocked her path. It gestured wildly with its index finger, pointing toward the alley she had just passed.

She debated kicking it. Yet, for some indistinct reason, she found herself checking her watch instead. The timepiece was an old theme park relic, with a mascot whose hands had long since degraded into bulbous nubs. She had about thirty minutes to spare. Against her better judgment, she walked in the indicated direction.

As she entered the alley, a sound like rain on hard stones rose around her. But it wasn't rain. The alley wasn't littered with trash or loose cobble. It was littered with skittering hands. All disembodied. All different—ranging in size, shape, and motion. There were gnarled dockworker hands. There were some with slim, elegant fingers like ballerinas' legs.

With practiced ease, she gently rubbed her fingers against her opposite forearm. Beneath each nailbed, a single rosethorn curled outward from the soil of her flesh.

If the hands made a move for her, she would cut them. Not deeply—just enough to show she meant business.

Could you kill a hand? Would it bleed out? Or did they exist separately from bodies and their rhythms—heartbeats and pulses?

Instead of swarming over her, they began to form a clump, climbing into and over one another, linking together into a growing tower of flesh and knuckles. Hands branched to form the suggestion of an arm. Then chest, hips, the swelling of a belly, and shoulders. Then a face, forming eyes from the O's of forefingers and thumbs, then nose, lips, even a suggestion of hair.

When all the hands were at last combined together, the 'man' made of hands regarded her. As the mouth-fingers pantomimed, the hands began to sign.

"You want me to follow you?" she guessed.

It had no eyes. No ears. Could it see her at all? Maybe it sensed motion? Vibration?

The hand-creature smiled: a thumb arced in dimples against ring-finger cheeks. It waved for her to follow and began down the alley, taking one halting step after another.

It was a short walk. The hand-creature led her, lumbering cheerfully through back alleys and side streets. Even when they crossed wide thoroughfares, no one looked twice.

Maybe they didn't see anything strange.

Maybe they just didn't want to get involved.

Laurel wondered if she had ever passed someone like this herself—someone led by a creature, elf, or fairy. A thing made of hands.

They stopped, ironically, at a store marked with a palm reader logo. The creature didn't unlock the door, exactly. Instead, multiple open hands—emerging from tentacle-like ropes of other hands—slotted perfectly into eight palm prints carved into the doorway. A click.

Laurel turned as a section of the alley's cobbled floor popped up to reveal a narrow spiral staircase downward.

One thought said run. The other—the louder—said bury yourself. Go down. She did. The creature dropped its humanoid façade, disassembling into hundreds of separate hands that went clattering and slithering past her and down, down, down.

The chamber below was a shop of palms reading—not palm reading, but palms reading.

In addition to the ones she'd come with, hundreds of disembodied hands littered the room, perching on shelves or sitting at tables, skimming braille scrolls and books with delicate concentration.

At the center sat a figure on a massive oak throne, dulled and de-gilded by age. He was clothed in hands. His robe—stitched with hundreds, maybe thousands. But something told Laurel there were far more than met the eye. Space bent strangely around him, folding in infinite pockets and seams, storing digits in layers like creased fabric.

He looked up. His eyes were green like ancient moss set in a face like a decaying stump.

"I appreciate your willingness to come with my servants," began the Man of Many Hands. His voice was layered, not quite one voice but many. One moment old and rasping, the next high and lilting. "I've been doing some reading on your situation. Quite the interesting curse you have."

Laurel didn't ask anything foolish like *Why me?* or *What do you want?* Instead, she simply watched, feeling the pressure inside her ribs.

"That must be uncomfortable," the man said, tapping his chest with a hand that had eight pointer fingers sprouting from one wrist. "You don't have much time left. But I'm willing—we're willing—to offer you assistance. I believe I can break your curse within the month. Ample time before next spring... and before you bloom into... well, I needn't say more."

Laurel knew it was true. She could feel the flowering coming soon. Maybe she'd make it one more season. Maybe not. The worst part wasn't the bark, or the sap, or even the buds that sometimes bloomed in her sleep. It was the waiting. The not-knowing. If it would end with a scream, or just a slow withering. If she'd matter when it was done.

Maybe she'd go the way her mother had—without goodbye. Blooming into a riot of peonies and potatoes and wormwood and donkeytail succulents.

Maybe, like Daphne, she'd become the tree her name suggested: Laurel.

But would that be so bad?

What else did she have? Odd jobs and side hobbies. She'd learned to solve a Rubik's cube, decode Morse, play chess, change a tire, cook a professional sauce, program computers, even craft foam art. She told herself it was curiosity, but really, she just wanted to be the kind of person who could be noticed. As if knowing things, doing things, might anchor her. Might let her outpace the roots that crept beneath her skin. All of it in hopes something—anything—might help her bloom on the outside, too.

"All I need," said the Man of Many Hands, "is a handshake. Your word that once I've broken your curse, you will give me both of your hands. Painlessly, of course. I am, after all, a collector of rare and... in your case, *verdant* oddities. I have never failed to get what I want."

And she believed it.

She felt the bark begin to thicken across her sternum again, quiet as breath. What if, she wondered... what if.... Her fingers curled into his as if answering a question she hadn't meant to ask. The deal was struck before she even realized her hand had moved.

He grinned wild, the extra fingers on his palm wrapped all the way up her forearm. "A deal is made."

Oscar King IV is a Bay Area-based English teacher and writer whose work draws from global stories of resistance, fairy tales, and finding wonder in the mundane. When he isn't working with emerging writers, he's likely solving some new riddle or reading first drafts to his two dachshunds. Discover more at OscarKingIV.com

Children's and YA

Category Winner:
The Water Bank: Tales of Innocence
by E.B. Wagner

CHAPTER ONE

The man whom I called Father had once said that children were the most fruitful investments. In auspicious times, you could raise them smart; a good job brought good water. In dire times, you could sell them fast; a young body brought even better water. As I stared at that man's funerary jar, at the sixty-seven liters of water that used to be his body, and that were now contained in a six-foot-tall transparent glass tank, I wondered, if only for a second, whether I was mourning the man or the missed opportunity to collect sixty-seven liters of water.

At this unfilial thought, I tightened my crossed arms around my chest and buried my fingers into the edges of my shoulders. Trying to quiet my mind, I closed my eyes and took a deep breath laced with the woody smoke of the pine incense stick that burnt on the altar, upon which the funerary jar had been placed.

"Father," I said, forcing myself to make my voice clear. "For the past year, I have avenged you."

As I spoke, scenes flashed before my eyes, tainted with the bluish hue of electric weapons and the smell of burnt flesh. I hung onto them, leaned into them, as I felt a reassuring rush of warm hatred blooming in my chest. Slowly, I looked up once more into the water tank before me. In the circular glass, I met the reflection of my own gaze—two phoenix eyes with their outer corners swept upwards, the color of a century-long frozen lake lying untouched in the tundra, testament to my maternal lineage. The candlelight barely reached their depths, instead highlighting my thin, pale face framed by silver hair, the same shade as that of the man whose liquified remains I was staring into.

"Father," I resumed, "Today, as I honor you, I must revel with the last of those who betrayed our family. Please take no offense. Tomorrow, I will rid our city of these traitors, and we will have our vengeance." My voice settled into a calm whisper. "And I will be free."

Hearing a faint clamor coming from the depths of the temple, I slowly wiped off the half-dried tears on my cheeks with the lace of my glove.

"Milady," a female voice echoed behind me, "the games are about to start."

Sandaled steps barely resonated behind my back, soft against the marble, characteristic of the trained gait of the Creation's priests. Not even the flames of the candles wavered on the altar as they came forth. Before me, the glass of my father's funerary jar reflected the shine of the gold powder that the priests applied on their shoulders, so that I could discern two hesitant silhouettes lining up with boxes in their arms and an armor stand hovering by their side.

"Lady Colona," the voice grew nervous, "your uncle demands your presence."

Reluctantly, I crossed my arms over my chest and lowered my head in one last bow before rising from my kneeling position. With practiced indifference, I glanced at the lad and maiden whose sheer white togas fell to the ground in elaborate wraps of silk, yet barely covered their gold-powdered chests. Their luscious hair, unrestrained, cascaded down their bodies to their lower backs in the style customary to their functions. Their appearance would have been impeccable, if not for the fact that they lacked the painted lines of the Creation's golden halo on their forehead.

Unordained priests, I thought, and my jaw clenched at the insult. *The High Priestess can't wait for tomorrow, it seems.*

The two young adults bent low in a full bow before bringing forth the armor stand, a mannequin of metal decked in an opaque helmet and white unitard. The pulse of the thruster under its feet seemed to echo increasingly loudly in the quiet room as I forced myself into a still position. I watched the priests-to-be enter my personal space and felt trembling fingers unbuttoning my gown, pearl after pearl. Sewn in the trapezoidal shape of a traditional *sarafan*, made of white lace over white silk with a pattern of Siberian irises and bluebells, the dress was buttoned down from my neck to my toes.

"We will be here all morning with those shaky hands of yours," I said with a cold voice, looking down at the maiden crouched at my feet.

Panic flashed through her eyes. "Pardon me, Milady," she hurriedly said, her hands shaking even more. "Please don't liquefy me!"

"Liquefy you?" I repeated, taken aback.

As I uttered those words, the reason for her fright dawned on me, and I let out a breath of dry laughter.

"The priests who were liquified on my orders were traitors to the Water Bank. Are you a traitor?"

She repeatedly shook her head, kneeling on the ground with her face against the marble floor and her gray hair scattered around her. Judging from her fleshy body and plump skin, she contained about forty liters and had never known thirst. She probably was an eleventh or twelfth child. Perhaps the parents had pushed her towards the clergy to pay penance. Would the need to sell a few arise, they had enough children to ensure wealth. Too bad she had apparently skipped her preceptors' lectures on the methods for quieting one's spirit.

"Milady, I am not ordained yet. Only ordained priests and priestesses may tend to those neither related by blood nor by marriage," she recited. "If, by skin-to-skin contact, I altered the moisture of Milady's body, I would be liquefied—"

"Enough," I interrupted. Having my body's moisture brought into the conversation was already more than a sufficient reason to put an end to it. Reciting the Statutes of the Water Bank without exercising situational awareness was another reason. "You are here on the High Priestess's orders. Get up and prepare my bodysuit."

I turned to the lad who had been unbuttoning the cuffs of my puff sleeves.

"You," I called, "your hands are not trembling. Take her place."

Obediently, the young man kneeled in front of me while his colleague hastily retreated to the armor stand. Unlike that teary-eyed girl, he kept a mask of calmness over his dainty features, creating quite a contrast between inner maturity and apparent youthfulness. Now that he came closer, I noticed the vividness with which his green eyes shone, and the rare warmth and opacity of his brown skin tone. Though he was on the scrawny side, without more than thirty-five liters of water in him, even the blackness of his hair displayed a depth of color.

"You were not born in a city-tower," I observed. "You were raised under the sun."

His hands, powdered with the gold of the Creation, briefly paused at the hem of my dress.

"Indeed." He knew better than to raise his gaze at me, so I could not see his expression, but I discerned a biting pride in his voice—the pride you cling to when it's all you have left, I thought. "My family was forced to move from the southern steppes to Mega when I was a child."

"The southern steppes are known for their dried-up lakes," I recalled. "Your moving must have been part of the Water Bank's campaign to bring the remaining ground populations into the safety of the city-towers."

As I spoke, his thin fingers resumed their unbuttoning of my *sarafan*.

"Milady is correct," he answered, and got up on his feet to unbutton the upper part of the garment, his eyes resolutely focused on his work, his face schooled into polite detachment.

In the quiet of the temple, I could hear the clamor growing louder outside, permeating through the marble walls and high ceiling as if it surrounded the building.

"Since you've lived in Mega for a while, I assume today's public games won't be your first," I resumed. His hands now worked their way up over my chest, revealing skin without ever touching it.

"They will be my first with Milady as a contestant," he gave me a smile that didn't reach his eyes. "People came from the five city-towers of the banking consortium to watch Milady fight and attend tomorrow's ceremony. Some even say..."

He trailed off as he unbuttoned the last pearl of my lace collar, and the sarafan fell at my feet. A cool draft caressed my bare skin, and I repressed a shiver.

"Well?" I asked with impatience.

His eyelids barely twitched, and he already turned his green gaze down before my body.

"Some of our patrons say that the name of our tower's new director will be announced at the ceremony," he uttered, with a prudent bow towards my father's funerary jar. "They say the winner of the games today will become the new director tomorrow."

E.B. Wagner is an attorney based in San Francisco and Paris. She writes young and new adult stories, mainly with science fiction themes. She has notably written two unpublished manuscripts with stories set in the same universe, one of which is *The Water Bank: Tales of Innocence*. Find more of her work at EBWagner.com.

Home Is Where the Cauldron Is
by Blair Visscher

Emma didn't know which was worse – being chased down by an evil wizard bent on killing her or wet socks. As she felt the wet squish of her pruned foot in her tight wet socks sink into her soaked Converse sneakers, she thought perhaps wet socks was winning. Then she returned her focus to muttering a spell of invisibility. It required constant repetition because she had added in an untraceable spell, but she wasn't far along enough in her studies to know how to cast it for any length of time. So, she cast it over and over and over under her breath as she squished down the side of Birch Street in the middle of the night in the pouring rain. She mostly succeeded in ignoring the yowling and moaning coming from the heavy bag on her back. She just needed to reach her great Aunt's house. Then she would be under the protection spell of the house, and she wouldn't need to worry about evil wizards or wet socks.

She turned up Willow Lane, her legs aching in pain from walking for the last four hours. There was the gate in the distance. Emma refused to let herself feel any relief yet. Not until she was safe inside the house. She squished past the lavender hedges and pushed on the old metal gate. It was locked. Feeling exasperated, Emma stood for a moment muttering and trying to also decide what to do. Should she pause in her efforts to open the lock? Surely a thirty-second pause so close to safety would be okay. Her backpack yowled, and she winced as claws dug into her back. Decision made, she stopped muttering, whispered an unlocking spell, swung the gate open, and stepped inside.

Immediately, a warm energy enveloped her. If she concentrated enough, it looked like green sparkles shimmering all around the house up to the gate and the hedge. She was safe. Looking up at the house she hadn't visited for seven years, not since she was six years old, she sighed in relief. Though it was dark and raining, the house looked as peaceful as she remembered. It had a steeply peaked roof with a brick chimney, whitewashed walls, and a light blue door and trim. The little covered porch offered a respite from the rain.

Emma ran up the steps and banged on the door, her memories flooding back to her. Baking cookies with her great Aunt, climbing the huge willow tree in the yard and swinging from the weeping branches. Feeling safe and happy.

The door swung slowly open. No lights were on. No Aunt Sophie stood to welcome her. Emma hesitated. She hadn't thought Aunt Sophie wouldn't be here.

"Hello?" she called into the house. Her backpack suddenly could not be contained. It erupted in a frenzy of hissing and yowling.

"Okay, okay! I know, geez, you're welcome for saving your life!" She stepped into the dry house and slung her bag to the ground. She crouched down to open the top of the bag, noticing both she and the backpack were leaving puddles spreading over the old oak floors.

A soaking wet black shadow leaped from the bag, hissing and spitting. It took off into the dark house.

"Don't wreck anything!" Emma called after it.

She reached into the bag and pulled out the only other thing in it. A thick old book. It was dry. Emma had suspected the book would look after itself, but she was relieved to find she was right. She had gone to a lot of trouble for this book.

She pulled off her wet shoes and socks, grimacing with distaste as her socks clung to her as if they didn't want to let go. She left them in the puddle – she'd have to clean that up soon- and added her jacket and sweater. Grabbing the book, she reached out to the wall to find a light switch, but before she could flick it on, a light down the hall glowed to life.

"Aunt Sophie?" Emma called as she walked past the steep staircase and down the narrow hall.

She reached the bathroom and saw that a candle on a sconce on the wall was lit.

Emma looked wildly around. "Hello?" She called again. Suddenly, the shower started up, fog starting to mist the mirror as warm water poured from the faucet. Emma realized it was the house. She hadn't known the house had this level of magic, but it made sense. Aunt Sophie was an extremely powerful witch, and her mother had been as well. She had lived here before Sophie. When witches stay and work magic in one place for that length of time, the place around them develops its own sort of magic. Emma needed no further prompting.

She finally felt warm after showering. Wrapped in a fluffy robe and wearing matching slippers with bunny ears on them, she wiped the fog off the mirror and looked at herself for the first time since her escape.

Her black hair was plastered to the sides of her head. Her grey eyes stared back at her and looked a lot less afraid than she really felt. Where was her Aunt Sophie?

There wasn't anything she could do about it tonight. Grabbing the old book, she opened the bathroom door, steam billowing out with her. A light shimmered at the end of the hall. The kitchen, if she remembered correctly. All Emma wanted to do was fall asleep, but she followed the light, knowing the house was guiding her and not wanting to be rude to a house.

The kitchen was bathed in candlelight, and rain lightly pattered on the windows behind cheerful curtains. On the island in the centre of the snug little kitchen was a mug of hot chocolate and a plate of chocolate chip cookies.

"Oh, thank you!" Emma squealed. She downed about half the mug in one gulp, suddenly realizing how hungry she was. She shoved two cookies in her mouth and grabbed the plate and mug.

"A girl could get used to this!" She turned, trying to decide where to sit. Light beckoned again from down the hall. Passing the bathroom, she walked by the front door. All signs of her puddle were gone along with her clothes. That's curious, she thought. How much power does the house have? How did it pick up clothes? She couldn't find it in her to be alarmed or worried. She knew she was safe and that the house was taking care of her, so she decided she didn't need to work out the how right now.

Through the entrance way was the living room. There was now a fire crackling in the hearth and a comfortable-looking pink reading chair pulled up to it. She knew the chair was there for her, but there was a black fluff of fur in the centre of the cushion. As she approached, it growled low.

"Don't start with me."

The growling stopped.

"Also, you're in my chair. It's big enough to share."

One eye opened and the black fluff glared at her.

Shrugging, Emma scooped it up and sat down, sighing. She placed her mug and plate and book on the perfectly placed side table and shoved the fluff in her lap. It immediately stood up and stared at her in disbelief. It was the first time since her escape Emma had been able to look at the baby dragon. It had black fluffy fur, a long black tail, and tiny, scaled wings. It bared its teeth at her, but Emma didn't react. She just held out a cookie. Cautiously, the dragon sniffed it and then grabbed it between its sharp, pointed teeth and flopped down on Emma to eat. She wasn't sure why she grabbed the creature when she was fleeing the wizard's lair, other than that she couldn't bear to leave it. It was too young to be away from its parents. Just like her.

"Tomorrow, we will find Aunt Sophie. And figure out what's in this book the wizard found so important. Tomorrow."

Emma slumped into the chair and felt her body begin to pull her down into the sleep she had been fighting for hours. She was warm, full, clean, and safe. But other than the dragon, she was alone. Her heart ached. Why the wizard had gone after her and her parents, she couldn't say. But she swore she would find out, and then they could all be together again. With this thought, she drifted into sleep.

Sunlight streamed into the living room, pulling Emma out of sleep. Hot dragon breath filled her nose, and she sputtered awake.

"Ew, why!?" She opened her eyes to see the dragon's green eyes staring into hers, only inches away. It smiled toothily at her.

"Okay, that is seriously creepy." She picked up the tiny dragon and put it on the ground.

A sharp knock sounded on the door.

Blair Visscher is a graduate student researching social media mis- and disinformation and its effect on behaviour during climate crises, in particular wildfire. In her free time, she loves to read and write inspiring stories about strong protagonists who save the world. She lives in the forests of Canada with her two children.

Ceramics and Secrets
by Chloe Kerr-Stein

Sunday, August 20th
Nina's House

This was a perfect moment.

Jules and Nina tangled up in Nina's cream-pink sheets, a bowl of popcorn on their collective lap. Nina's laptop sat across from them, playing some inane Netflix show. Something to do with love and baking cupcakes. It was gay, which was why they'd chosen it.

But Jules didn't really care what they were watching. She was with Nina, that's what mattered. After all these years, she was *with* Nina. Jules tilted her head, letting Nina's straight blond hair tickle her face. She cuddled in closer and kissed Nina's cheek, gently brushing away a lock of hair. Nina's gaze traveled from Jules's eyes to her mouth as she leaned in to close the gap between them.

Jules's breath caught as Nina's lips touched hers. She closed her eyes and let herself focus on the kiss. Maybe, if Jules were careful, she could make this moment last forever. But then the dull background noise of the TV show stopped, and Nina pulled away.

Are you still watching? The screen read.

Nina laughed. Jules joined her.

"*Are* we still watching?" Nina asked, shutting the laptop before flumping down next to Jules.

"I guess not." She tried to match Nina's light tone.

Jules turned her head to see Nina's expression, pressing her cheek up against a cushy pink throw pillow. It was difficult to read. Had Nina pulled away because the show suddenly paused or because she didn't want to make out right now? This was all so new—especially for Nina—and Jules didn't want to ruin it.

Lost in thought, Jules didn't notice Nina lean in for another kiss until their noses touched. This one was longer, and Jules let herself sink into it. She reached up and gently cupped Nina's face in her hand. The last bit of afternoon light filtered in through the window, filling the backs of Jules' eyelids with a warm glow. They sank into the pillows, arms wrapped around each other in a perfectly choreographed dance they'd been practicing all summer.

Nina pulled away just enough to whisper, "I'm going to miss this."

The words hit Jules with a thud. What did Nina mean, she would *miss* this? Sure, summer was ending, but they weren't saying goodbye. Except...that's what happened last summer. Without warning, memories flashed through Jules's mind. Unanswered texts and canceled plans. Passing Nina in the hallway, and her not even waving.

But this year would be different. This year, Jules reminded herself, she and Nina were more than friends.

"Yeah, me too." Jules managed to choke out.

"Ugh, I can't believe school starts tomorrow!" Nina groaned, letting her head hang limp against Jules's shoulder. Jules sat up a bit, angling her body so Nina could lie more comfortably.

"Me neither," Jules replied, wrapping her arms around Nina.

Nina twisted around to look at Jules, a smile playing across her face.

"I had a lot of fun this summer. Everything's easier when it's just the two of us."

"I know." The words tumbled out of Jules' lips easily. Because it was true. When it was just the two of them, Nina was a different person. She was Jules's favorite person. And from the way Nina looked at her when they were alone...the way she hung onto Jules's every word… Jules thought she might be Nina's favorite person, too.

But tomorrow was the first day of Junior year. They would be back at school, surrounded by Nina's snobby dance friends. What would keep Jules from fading into the background of Nina's life, just like she had for the last two years?

"So...tomorrow at school," she started, still not sure how she was going to phrase this. But then, she looked into Nina's hazel eyes, and the words just slipped out. "What are we going to tell people...about us?"

Jules's heart hammered inside her chest. She couldn't believe she'd just said that. Jules was *pretty* sure she could call Nina her girlfriend...but what if she was wrong?

Nina didn't answer right away. She turned to lean against Jules' chest.

"I told you at the beginning of the summer, I'm not ready to come out as anything yet."

Damnit. Jules had said the wrong thing.

"I know, I know!" She held Nina tighter, trying to erase her mistake. "And I'm not trying to pressure you or anything, or rush you to come out. I was just wondering… *if* we told people, eventually, when you're ready… what would we say? Like..." Jules felt a lump rising in her throat. Once she said the words, there was no going back. But she had to know. So Jules took a deep breath and finished her sentence. "Are you my girlfriend?"

A smile flickered around Nina's mouth.

"Oh," she said quietly. "Is that what you want? To be girlfriends?"

"Only if it's what you want!"

"Even though I'm not ready to come out?"

Jules's heart swelled. She imagined how confusing this must be for Nina. How overwhelming. Maybe that's why she'd always kept her distance at school. It wasn't because she cared less. It had been the opposite. She cared about Jules too much.

"Of course, Nina. It doesn't matter who we tell. I really like you, and I want to be your girlfriend."

Nina bit her lip.

"Really? Even though we'd have to keep it a secret?"

"Of course. I want you to come out on your own timeline. When you're ready. But I want to be your girlfriend, whether or not we're telling people about it."

Nina smiled.

"Okay then. We're girlfriends."

And then, they were kissing again, and all of Jules's fears were melting away. This year would be different. Because now, Nina was her girlfriend.

Chloe Kerr-Stein lives in San Francisco and writes queer coming-of-age stories with a focus on found family. She has an undergraduate degree in Writing and Literature from UC Santa Barbara. Chloe is currently working on edits for her first book.

Monarch

by Emily King

"Tonight is the most important night of my life," I say, looking over my reflection in the glass, "and I look like an overstuffed fireowl." My mane of red curls is as unruly as ever, cascading over the multiple layers of lace on the dress my mother designed.

"Technically, I think your birthday was the most important day of your life," Amberine mumbles from the floor, pins in her mouth.

"Well, this is a close second. Maybe third, if we count the time I rescued those baby robin-blues midair after Marigold accidentally toppled their nest."

Saying my sister's name makes my stomach tighten. I plant my feet into the ground and breathe, willing my grief to melt into the floor. I can't get distracted; not tonight. Even though the dress is abysmal, letting my mother choose my clothing gives her some semblance of control on nights like tonight; only a year ago, it was Marigold who was going into her challenge and preparing for her first migration.

Behind me, Amberine stands, then cocks her head.

"Well, for a *third* most important night, you don't look half bad. You look fancy. Plus, the dress is so ugly that it makes your wings really pop."

I groan. It's true; against the garish ball gown and my wild red hair, my Monarch wings look brighter than usual, more tangerine. As I move, the fabric Amberine had been pinning drops to the floor in a pathetic, *dramatic* puddle.

"Hold on," she says squatting down, "that's not supposed to happen." As she tries to adjust my hem, stabs my ankle with a needle.

"Dungbeetle!" I curse.

"Sorry! You know I'm not good at this. We could always call my dad."

"And risk him telling my mom that you're having to add another layer to this monstrosity because I smeared sketching charcoal all over it?" I lift a black-stained sleeve, then let it fall.

"Not a chance."

"Then stop complaining." She bites down on her sewing needle, gathering up the fabric before starting again. "And because I messed up the dress, I'll even let you talk through your nerves again. Even though that's all we talk about anymore...."

"You'll thank me next year when it's your turn," I say, gathering my thoughts. "Okay. The fairies who are creating the challenge tonight are the Emperor fairies. That means they have metal magic."

"And the last time the metal fairies issued a challenge it was—"

"Sword fighting. Each initiate had to craft a weapon from mud, and then their weapon was turned into steel by an Emperor. The first three to disarm each other won the challenge."

The first three. All I have to do is place in the top three; the top three initiates are given the honor of apprenticing the Prism Guard on the Great Migration.

"I hope it isn't any type of combat," I say. Especially if Mother insists I wear this. Once I win the challenge, *then* I'll be able to focus on honing my fighting skills. Prism apprentices are highly trained. They have to be.

"Well, what was the challenge when your aunt won?"

"Malachite fairies – so plant magic. Aunt Rose had to scale a tree so tall she couldn't see the top from the ground. No flying."

Amberine straightens, then steps back to look at me. "I did my best," she says apologetically.

Her added layer sags across my torso, barely covering the large black stains near my collar and on my midsection.

We are both frowning at my reflection when the needle and thread lift off the floor. They whip around my body and skirt, tightening and shifting the fabric until the stains are almost invisible. My stomach shifts with simultaneous relief and dread.

"That's better," Amberine's father, Iseli, says, leaning against the doorway. His own monarch wings are a pale peach, almost identical to his daughter's, were it not for the tear in Amberine's left one. He goes behind the counter and scans the rows of fabric on the wall before pulling down a gray shawl made of spider silk. "Put this on."

He tosses it to me and I wrap it around my arms, covering the last of the stain on my shoulder.

The shop door rings, and in walks... no, *strides*, a Prism Guard. My heart lodges in my throat as we bow to her; I didn't realize they had arrived already. The nerves I felt a few moments ago tidal wave across my skin as she walks toward me.

When I was seven, my aunt told me that Prism Guards were demi-gods and goddesses; that they were fairies who spent their lives protecting our home from the threats of the human realm and the realms beyond; that they were gifted by the goddesses with superior magic and the purest of hearts. I believed her, partly because the guards in their uniform all seemed to have a glowing aura about them, and partly because my aunt herself was one of them.

The fairy in front of us has wings banded with orange and yellow from base to hem, decorated with multiple intricate black-white patterns. Goddesses, Lacewing fairies are gorgeous. I envy those patterns almost as much as I envy her magic. *Animal magic.*

As she turns to me, I'm reminded of the drawing of the jaguar that I was sketching earlier—the same one that caused me to ruin my dress in the first place. A second set of eyes is painted on her eyelids so that even when she blinks, she is still staring at us.

Great; even with her eyes closed, she can still see my stupid outfit.

"Hello, Monarchs," the Lacewing says, voice like honeyfloss. "I'm sorry to be popping in so last minute, but on my flight over, my horned beetle accidentally ripped the jacket I'm supposed to be wearing to tonight's Migration ceremony."

Of course, she rides a horned beetle. Beyond epic.

"I can fix that," Iseli says, taking the jacket from her as she shrugs it off around her wings. "And welcome to the Citrine City, home of the Migrating Monarchs."

As Monarchs, it is our duty to distribute magic on our Great Migration. It's the Prism Guard's duty to put their lives on the line to protect the migrating Monarchs. I look at the fairy in front of me and hope I get to migrate as the protector, not just the protected.

"Moss here will see you there; she is competing in the challenge."

I try not to trip off the platform I'm standing on as I extend a hand.

"I'm Moss. I'm a huge fan of the Guard." She grips my hand and shakes it, the veins in her arm flexing. She has a tattoo of a polar bear on her bicep. I wonder if that's one of the animals she's seen on her trips to the human realm.

I know that the realm is full of more than animals. There are dangers there, too; beings like witches that will drain your lifeforce – that drained *Marigold's* lifeforce. That's why I need to become a guard. Not just for the glory—not just to devote my life to a noble cause—but to hunt down those who take advantage of our magic. And when I finally come into my magic on the Migration, I'll be ever more equipped to do that.

Of course, I don't dare say all that to her. There's more to being a Prism Guard than hunting down witches. "I've been wanting to join since I can remember," I manage. "My aunt was a guard. She's retired."

"I'm Fawnia. I hope you win the challenge; it'd be refreshing to have someone so eager on our team. A Monarch's first Migration is always a thrilling moment. Savor every second."

I squeeze down in excitement before it occurs to me I probably shouldn't still be holding her hand. I let go as Fawnia takes my place on the platform and puts her jacket back on, Iseli having repaired the rip during our brief conversation.

Amberine gives me an enthusiastic thumbs up as Fawnia gives herself a once-over in the mirror. I mock fainting and then give her a wave, backing towards the door.

"Oh, and Moss," the Lacewing calls before I leave. "Nice dress. Peacocking—smart move." She winks at me.

I make a mental note to thank my mother as I fly home.

The last thing she wants is for her daughter to become a Prism Guard, not after what happened to Marigold. She knows that she can't protect me from the human realm, not entirely. I may not be able to bring Marigold back, but I can do her justice by making sure no other lives are lost to quench the thirst of their rotting hearts. And when I come into my magic on the Migration, I'll be ever more equipped to do that.

I just have to win the challenge first.

Emily King is a writer, dance teacher, choreographer, and dachshund wrangler living in the Bay Area. Through both language and movement, she aims to "pour hot magic into spaces chilled with disbelief." She infuses her craft with eco-feminist themes and the whimsy she draws from her two daughters and her experiences teaching at an all-girls high school. Learn more at bit.ly/EmilyAKing and follow her on TikTok @twodachshundkings.

Ixle Island
by Kyra Ashwood

Scientists tell us the universe created organisms to recycle nutrients, but those same scientists claim they created new organisms to improve our food supply. If I were to create a new species, it would fly me through the winds, dive me through the waves, and entertain my little brothers through the winter. I suppose I'll find out soon if my creation shares any resemblance with the scientists' skilled tinkering of genetic material.

Frothy peaks in the lavender waves below me twirl much like my favorite frozen yogurt. Except instead of tickling my tongue, these waves would twist around me talon-like and tenderize my body before feeding me to the deep sea. I shift my eye away from the air hole and rest my head against the wall of the shipping crate, knees digging into the foam base. The crisp scent of mudelan wood tantalizes my nose with memories of the grove of trees at my city park, a tame space compared to what awaits me on Ixle Island.

I'm brave. I'm strong. I'm fine. This trip is fine.

The lump forming on the inside of my lip disagrees.

The racket of the drone propellers razes my thoughts, the harsh sound penetrating my ear shields. As long as it's still flying, I won't plummet. I quadruple-checked my arrival coordinates. No early landings for me.

I admit this trip was a bit impulsive. Not all of my ideas reflect the soundness of a debate, with long lists of the pros and cons. That process tends to stall my decisions, and I prefer to launch my mission first, form the battle plans while I'm in the air, and hope I land without too many bruises. But I don't normally take flights, and never packaged as cargo.

This adventure wasn't even my fault. My best friend Kenzie dared me to hack into the island's supply drone system; she assumed I'd decline. And I've only declined a dare twice: first when the timing conflicted with my little brother's birthday party, and second when I'd have to dance in front of the hottest guy at school.

Kenzie nearly disabled my workstation when I breached the last security barrier to the drone shipment log. And once I was in, my fingers moved on their own accord, without much input from my prefrontal cortex. Revised flight itinerary and crate drop-off location. I gave myself an hour to explore the island before the drone seals the crate to return. Sufficient time to make the dreadful hour airborne worth it, but not long enough to raise suspicions. I hope. A crew might wait to apprehend me the moment I emerge. If not, I claim bonus material to justify my late biology report and bragging rights for the next three, maybe six, years.

Once I hijack my gaze out of the grasp of the foamy swirls, the dusky sand of the approaching coastline forms a border, like a child separating the jungle from the sea in their drawing. Two blinks later, the sand spreads out below, its smooth surface disturbed by glistening oblong stones, a thousand predatory pupils glaring at the sky. What I would give to curl up on a towel down there and sip an icy glass of gulela nectar, its sugary goo sliding over my tongue while the gentle waves wash over my toes. My mom might be up for it; she craves a little adventure in the summer. Though she usually dumps me with Grandma when she travels.

My next blink and towering trees replace the short beach, their velvety leaves concealing the understory. If any of the island's beasts roam this jungle, their secrets persist camouflaged from my illegal stares. No one views the island researchers' creations without a wallet as deep as this sea or a few strings on the politicians' hands. Except a fifteen-year-old girl who spends too much of her life sucked into the intraverse network at the science academy, coercing words and symbols to bend to her will. Some call it coding, some call it hacking; I call it bridging the information gap between the scientists who run everything and the rest of us.

Several minutes of jungle dissolve into a blur of tangled greens not unlike the salad I ate for lunch, which wasn't nearly enough food in advance of this journey. My hands ache from leaning against the side of the crate, holding myself at a proper viewing angle. Finally, patches of emerald ponds and clumped shrubs replace the trees.

The drone lowers the crate into the grass, removes the top of the crate, and lands nearby. I slip on my sunglasses as sunlight floods my dark cell. The hot air coils around my bare arms and legs, piercing my pores with its moisture.

The empty clearing may be the loneliest place I've visited, without any birds flying past or insects buzzing around. In the opposite direction from the trees, the grasses thin out until jagged rocks jut out of the land like my worst acne nightmare, their copper spirals ready to pierce the unfortunate drone with incorrect landing coordinates. A tingle of adrenaline seeps through me. I'm here! I did it!

I set the timer on my watch for fifty-five minutes, a little buffer to ensure I don't screw up. The drone will plop that lid back on with or without me and return home.

I drop from the edge of the crate wall and land softly on the knee-height yellow grass below, my hiking boots squishing a smidge into the soil. I stride towards the rocky spirals, my hands hooked around the shoulder straps of my bag, lest I grab a poisonous plant and have an allergic reaction. This island is infamous for its animals, but that doesn't mean they aren't also modifying the plants.

Sweeping expanses of crimson soil replace the grass long before I reach the rocks. Footprints dart everywhere, the worst a monstrosity longer than my foot with three toes, the nails drilling down so deep I wouldn't be surprised if some insect inhabits the gashes in the soil. I squat to snap a photograph and trace my finger along the edge of the indentation. Until finding this footprint, so unlike any known animal, I half-convinced myself this island differs little from the rest of the mainland.

But no, secret species roam this island. And their lax security can't even prevent an unwelcome visitor's arrival. A tiny snake of a thought twists its way through my head, constricting around every firing neuron with a worry worse than being arrested: finding myself cornered by some monster with no people left here to rescue me.

Or no one who would want to rescue me. I've heard some of these scientists will guard their secrets against any threat.

Kenzie warned me this trip was a terrible idea.

I'm fine. This footprint has dried, its owner long departed. No one is shooting at me. I'm fine.

I force myself not to flee when I stand up. A small transport skycraft silently lands a thirty-second dash away. With forty-two minutes left on my timer, even if I beat them back to my drone, I'd still be stuck here. Plan A dissolved into dust. Up next would be Plan B, except I was too distracted sea-gazing to brainstorm. Beg forgiveness? I could offer up my mom's surgical expertise. But she's less forgiving.

While I debate my potential punishments, a lady in black pants and a button-up, collared shirt drops down from an exit hatch in the side of the skycraft. She smiles and waves. The dude who follows, with multiple guns strapped to his broad waist and back, scans the horizon before motioning the lady towards me. She must be here to ensure he doesn't hurt me when he hauls me in for questioning. Or lockup. Or feeding to the hungriest predator. Or however they punish trespassers.

Maybe Kenzie was right. But I always like to prove myself. Brave, bold, inquisitive.

My words. My mom's description leans towards impulsive, maybe downright stupid.

"Zinnia!" The lady shouts when she's a few steps away. "Thank God you're all right! Your mom has been worried sick, especially after your transmitter died and the security team reported your last coordinates. What are you doing out here? You only brought one backpack? Where are your supplies? Never mind, let's get you back."

She wraps her arm around my shoulders in a half-hug I suspect is meant to comfort me as she herds me towards the skycraft. I bite my tongue, debating whether I can outmaneuver the guy's still holstered guns or if I should follow my curiosity.

I haven't met Zinnia.

My name is Hazel, but my friends call me Haze. My mom is at the hospital replacing some old woman's hip, but she rarely knows my location and never worries about me. And while the unkept hair blowing free of the lady's ponytail reminds me of my chemistry teacher, I definitely haven't met these people.

Kyra Ashwood is a data scientist and researcher. She holds a PhD in ecology. Her stories aim to spark teen girls' interest in science and math. KyraAshwood.com

Fairshade
by Oscar King IV

Ellelle slid open her bedroom window, exalting in the spray of fog and the cold, skittery feeling that the ghostlight made on her exposed shoulders. It was a good night for... well, not treason *technically*, though that's what her mother would call it if she found out. What was the right word for 'sneaking refugees past border guards'? Bray would know.

Her window stared over a seventy-foot drop into the streets below. They were full of people even though the sun had long since set. Nights in the ghostlit city were more pleasant than the brutally hot days, but something in the darkness felt... odd. The air was brisk and full of unspent static. She mounted the windowsill, swung one leg, then the other, over the void. She uncorked a vial of something dark, drank it, then jumped.

She didn't even feel the rushing wind of her fall: the concoction she'd ingested flared in her. Power welled. As the ground sped to meet her, she was already tapping her new stores of magic.

As though crystallizing from the night, her magic materialized under her feet in a long, thin slide. The substance, gloomglass, hung steady in the air; she caught it underfoot and skimmed frictionlessly along it towards the city proper. She leaned into a curve, tilting toward one of the high houses on the edge of the northernmost island. Her magic drew a path into existence scant inches ahead of her while, in her wake, it dissolved into nothing.

As she skated through the air, she found it hard to imagine what Enviece had looked like before the seas had drained away. According to legend, it had once sat upon the ocean. A grand port city made of dozens of smaller and larger islands, all interwoven with water channels. Instead of airboats—with their thundering engines and whirring propellers—the city had been sailed by gentle gondolas trailing colored ribbons. Tonight, even under the blue haze of ghostlight that flooded everything, the fogs that filled the vast chasms looked nothing like water.

She crouched low and made her course a bit sharper, trying to pick up speed. Any minute now, her group would start the crossings. And if she wasn't there to help, well, there was just that higher of a risk for Enviece to gain new ghosts.

She didn't have to worry about being seen—in her dark outfit, she'd be barely a shadow against the night's mottled blues and black—not until she reached the chasms. Lighters would be on patrol, and if they saw her using thaumaturgy, they would kill her on sight.

Or, they'd try.

When she reached the western gorge, she dropped down a slow spiral of gloomglass into an alleyway. Though anyone could cross the city's islands in the daylight, at sunset, the city's massive bridges unwound like plants growing in reverse; at night, the lighters were strict about allowing people to move between the island districts without very explicit authorization. Unless, of course, you were a thaumaturge: a heretic who'd turned from the Light's good graces and embraced the goddesses' dark powers.

Ellelle surveyed the gorge before her. Though most of the airboats had been docked for the night, several flat-bottomed, rust-ribbed vessels patrolled the rivers of fog. Each one was manned by guards: gold buttons and gold trim and patterning that made their vests look adorned with dozens of unblinking gold eyes. Lighters. While one worked the engine, the rest manned wide, golden searchlights. Truelights.

If even a glimmer of that light touched her while she had concoction in her system, it would shatter *her* like glass. She'd seen it happen. Not pretty. Not survivable.

When the boat passed, she leapt into the chasm. Her power gave her a quick, sweeping path to the other side.

Her destination was a small house wedged between taller structures—findable only if you already knew it was there.

As she entered the hidden door, an exasperated groan greeted her. Lucarius smacked his forehead with a thwack. "Damnit, Ellelle, you're explicitly *not* on tonight's list."

"I know." She bowed theatrically, delighting in the tall, dark-haired young man's deepening frown. "You're welcome."

Lucarius was counting rows of orderly vials in a small crate. "If you wanted in, you should've come to the last three meetings. You can't keep showing up unannounced."

"Yeah, but you talk so much at those things. What have we here?" She lifted and peered into one of the vials. "This doesn't look like gloomglass."

"You took the last of the gloomglass two weeks ago," said the other young man in the room. Unlike his fraternal twin, who was angular and thin, Bray was thick and round everywhere; his haphazardly styled golden hair was a stark contrast to his tanned skin and orderly suit. He sat at a table that was covered in papers etched with a strange language. Math, Ellelle realized. "The alchemist hasn't been able to reproduce a stable batch since you took our last five vials."

"Five vials?" Lucarius exclaimed. "Ellelle, *that* is another reason you weren't on our list tonight: you keep burning through our supply. Every ounce of concoction that you use risks exposing us to the lighters."

She clicked her tongue. "I'm better than your next five thaumaturges combined. So what if I burn a little extra?"

"I know you're not using it just for the crossings. I know you're keeping some for yourself. And that jeopardizes–"

"Anyway," Ellelle interrupted, forcing her way past him to Bray's table, "how many refugees are we talking about tonight?"

"Early estimate is two dozen people. Could be all adults. Could be whole families. It's all gotten rather dicey."

She whistled through her teeth. "Why so many?"

"They're fleeing the conflict in the southern city-states in droves. And the numbers are only going to increase." Bray finally looked up, slipping off his glasses. Goddesses, he looked tired. "Tonight, the fogs are low. Lighters are hungry for action. And there are nearly a hundred automata on patrol."

"Sounds like they're on edge. Like they'll follow a diversion," Ellelle said.

"You're not putting yourself at risk again," Lucarius warned.

"It's not a risk. I'm too good. Even with two dozen to take."

"You were on the last crossing! You were on the one before that. *And* the one before that."

"And the one before that," Bray noted.

"So I'll take a little bit less concoction this time," she offered. "How's just three vials of...ugh, is this fellswim?"

"It's not just about the amount you take," Bray said softly.

"Every time you go out there," Lucarius continued, "you're rolling the dice on your life. You are good, but everyone slips up eventually."

"I don't," she said. It wasn't bragging. It was just true. "Every time I'm out there, it means more people get in; more people get to have something *resembling* safety in our city."

The guys shared a look. "Even so, this one's our turn," Lucarius snapped.

She laughed. "You're both terrible with anything but augmore."

"No, we're definitely better than average. We're just not freaks like you."

"Freakishly talented, you mean?"

"Yes," Bray added.

Ellelle smirked, then lifted a vial to her lips.

"Don't you *dare* double-dose. I know you're using gloomglass. I can see it in your eyes." Bray turned to Ellelle, seconding his twin's concern. "Second dosing *is* risky."

Ellelle considered the mixture. Fellswim was not ideal. But there were people out there who needed her. Who relied on her powers. Hell, there was a person right here who relied on her power. She was already holding it. She couldn't not take it now.

She uncorked the vial and downed the contents. The shock hit: she staggered, then steadied, letting the wave of new magical power bloom inside her. It was harsher than when she took gloomglass back at her window. Two dosages of separate concoctions really was rough. She grit her teeth and waited until the burn became a slow simmer, then just the hum of power.

Lucarius swore under his breath.

"Maybe I am putting myself at risk. Maybe I will slip eventually. Maybe I do just like the thrill. *Maybe* I am doing this because *she* would hate it," Ellelle said, exhaling. She gathered up her dark hair and tied it back in a tight bun. "But two dozen people are out there tonight hoping the world still has a place for them. And I don't want to be the reason they find out it doesn't."

"Listen," Lucarius said, making a grab for her. She slipped out of his grip, her arm fuzzing to smoke where he held her.

"Forty-five minutes," she said, beginning to sink into the floor. The sensation was like swimming in lukewarm ink. Her body entered the solid material easily, and she relished the odd wet-but-not-wet feeling. "South patrol. I'll have them all... occupied.

Don't worry. I have a good feeling about tonight." She turned toward the door, then disappeared into the earth.

Oscar King IV is a Bay Area-based English teacher and writer whose work draws from global stories of resistance, fairy tales, and finding wonder in the mundane. When he isn't working with emerging writers, he's likely solving some new riddle or reading first drafts to his two dachshunds. Discover more at OscarKingIV.com

Andrea Jones and the White Salon
by Patrik Lundh

*They thought I was a Surrealist, but I wasn't. I never painted
dreams. I painted my own reality.* ~ Frida Kahlo

CHAPTER ONE

Andrea was staring at a human skull discarded among the dead leaves beneath a gnarly oak tree. Who, she wondered, was the person whose eyes had once filled those empty eye sockets?

She heard the toilet flush. Then, over the whirring of an electric toothbrush, her father calling from the bathroom. "Ah ooh wedy?"

She was not ready. In fact, she decided, she wasn't going. She did not want to spend one more moment standing in front of her mother's grave, pretending to grieve.

Her attention returned to the oak tree, whose branches twisted through the air and cast their tentacled shadows across the human bones scattered near the skull. Below the ground, the oak's black roots wrapped like the fingers of a monstrous hand around a giant heart the color of rancid milk. The heart bulged limply in the roots' grip, and blood trickled from places where root tips had punctured the sickly surface, running in crimson-brown rivulets down the wall and pooling on the hardwood floor.

Her father spit and ran the faucet. "We need to go! It's gonna rain soon!"

Andrea dropped her brush in the pail and stepped over to the other side of the hallway to take in the entire scene. It was the largest image she'd painted so far, floor to ceiling. She'd had to unscrew the coat rack from the wall and shove the shoe bins out of the way to make space for it.

Scanning the walls, she realized there was no surface left to paint. Could that really be it? Had she finally finished painting every room in the apartment?

Except, of course, for one.

When Andrea thought about *that* room, her chest tightened, and the air in her throat stopped moving as if it had turned into cement. A sense of fury escaped from her gut and dispersed through her body like shards of glass. She was about to put her foot through the wall in anger, but managed to grasp for the only useful tool she'd retained from her many hours in therapy. She closed her eyes and mouth, placed the index and middle fingers on each side of the bridge of her nose, and covered her nostrils with her thumb and ring finger. Then, she breathed in and out through alternating nostrils until the beast loosened its grip and let her go.

In the bathroom, the faucet knobs squeaked and the water stopped running. The light switch clicked. Footsteps approached and stopped near enough for Andrea to hear her father's deep, familiar sigh.

"Um," he said. "Were you up all night again? Where are the shoes?"

The only room she hadn't painted, Andrea thought, was her mother's study. The room she'd never even been inside.

"I'm not going," Andrea said, her eyes still closed.

Quiet followed.

Andrea pictured her father, hands on hips, chin raised, eyes to the ceiling, swallowing some words, weighing others.

"Okay," he said. "Why?"

Because she was done with the charade. "I have a math test," she said.

Another pause. "Um," her father said. "Didn't Ms. Lubalin…that's your math teacher, right? I thought she said it'd be okay. It's your mother's birthday."

"She forgot. About the test."

"Ah." Her father sighed and shifted his feet. He cleared his throat. "Sweetie." He tapped her on the shoulder. "Can you open your eyes? When we talk?"

"I'm thinking."

Another sigh. "Right. Listen. I understand visiting your mother is still… difficult. If you really don't want to, you don't have to go. But. Can we talk about maybe seeing Lisa again? Or we can find someone else, if you want. I'm just worried about you, sweetie. It's just…it's been a while. You know?"

Three years, to be exact, since a police officer and a social worker had knocked on the door to their San Francisco flat to tell them that the search for Andrea's mother and Barry, Andrea's best friend Daniel's father, had been called off. The phrases "given the extreme conditions", "no one can survive," and "we're so very sorry" clung to Andrea's memory like smoke damage to wallpaper. The taste of spaghetti with Bolognese sauce she'd just finished eating had turned into a metallic coating in her mouth. The television sound of the baseball game she'd been watching with her father seemed to continue, inning after inning, while Andrea cried into her father's neck, feeling his warm tears on her face and his heavy sobs pushing against her ribs. At night, the thickness of grief felt glued into the air as if the universe had stopped breathing.

But her sorrow was short-lived. When told more details about what had happened, her sad feelings yielded to confusion and anger. Didn't it seem, she started thinking, that her mother, the brilliant neuroscientist, had simply come up with a final, ultimate excuse to stay away from her family? To be rid of her daughter for good?

Andrea had tried to talk to her father about her skepticism. She'd brought her questions to him, wrapped in the turbulent feelings that kept her up at night. But when her father threw away the wrapping and answered her questions with paternal repetitions of the authorities' official explanations, which she had come to believe were false, Andrea began to hide her thoughts about the whole affair. Instead, her misgivings continued to propagate in the dark of her mind, like pale potato sprouts in the back of the cupboard.

"Sure," Andrea said. "Maybe I should talk to Lisa again."

Her father took a deep breath. "Good. I'll email her. I think it'll help."

Andrea listened to her father walk around, retrieving the shoe bins she'd stuffed into the broom closet. She recognized the sound of cotton sliding against leather and could tell her father was putting on his ankle-high boots. The crinkle of nylon as he put on his rain jacket. The pause as he considered whether to extend an offer of affection in the form of a cautious hand on her shoulder, since the chasm between them these days rarely countenanced hugs.

It was amazing how much of the world she could infer through her imagination. She wondered what it would be like to be blind, to see only with your ears and nose and fingers.

"Okay," her father said. "I'm going. Sure you don't want to come?"

Andrea nodded.

As her father descended the stairs to the front door, he called out, "Good luck with your math test!"

When the front door closed, Andrea opened her eyes. Once again, she found herself staring at the skull and its empty eye sockets.

Where do minds go when they leave our bones behind? Her mother had said once when they happened upon a deer carcass during one of their yearly family camping trips to the Sierra Nevada mountains.

Or when they leave their daughters behind, Andrea had silently added.

Andrea turned her head and looked past the entry to the living room on the left, toward the window at the end of the hall. Her gaze lingered for a moment on the gray light filtering through the curtains before tilting to the right, where the doorframe of her mother's study loomed.

She pursed her lips, kicked the crate of painting supplies out of the way, and took several resolute steps in the direction of the study. But once standing in front of the door, her resolve faltered. She leaned against the opposite wall, slid down, and slumped on the floor, pulling up her knees and wrapping her arms around them.

She wasn't allowed to go inside.

Looking at the door, Andrea again felt like she was sinking into a pit of despair with nothing but walls of moving sand to climb to avoid plunging into its darkness.

Averting her gaze from the door, she noticed the myriads of question marks painted inside blue flames spewing from the door frame. She cringed at her own dilettantish handiwork, accomplished three years ago when she thought her mother's "death" meant she could finally enter the study to see what her mother had been working on, what had been so much more important than being with her family, and her father had said no. He had started inventing excuses for why they could not go inside. The door had been locked, and he said he couldn't find the key. Then, he said it was too soon to go inside, that he wasn't emotionally ready. Next, he said he planned to convert the room into an art studio for him and Andrea, except he needed to first clear it out. Eventually, the foot-dragging turned into a holding pattern, and the holding pattern calcified into mutual paralysis.

How could these thoughts and feelings that she couldn't see or touch raise barriers as impenetrable as steel?

Not anymore, she decided.

Patrik Lundh grew up in Sweden, exploring the blueberry forests surrounding his hometown, swimming in small lakes, and devouring books that inspired his dreams of becoming an author. He earned a Ph.D. in cultural anthropology at U.C. Santa Cruz and currently conducts social science research in education. Patrik lives in Berkeley. When he's not working, parenting, or baking bread, he loves to compose songs on his guitar and, most of all, write young adult science fiction novels.

Lying in Plainview
by Rebecca Lang & Jennie Burke

EASTER SUNDAY
The cemetery was quiet, the musky smell of freshly turned earth overwhelming in the evening air. The days were getting longer, and the sun angled through the trees, casting stretched shadows among the gravestones. A somber teen knelt to touch the temporary steel marker etched with their friend's name—the permanent headstone wouldn't be ready for months.

What epitaph would sum up this life— a life gone too soon, too suddenly? How could a few words give shape to a whole person?

Beloved

Adored

Forever in our hearts

Remembered with love

Lying in peace

And lying in Plainview, forever.

A fat tear dropped to the dirt.

"I wish I could bring you back." The words wriggled out, like bugs from the underside of a rock.

How could so much go wrong over the course of a week?

Countless lies and heartache.

There was so much to tell and a thousand ways to begin, but let's start with last Monday, and The List....

MONDAY — *6 Days Earlier*
Abby took her time fixing her lip gloss before clicking off her phone and looking up at Mr. Dewar, standing over her desk.

"Abilene." He used his teacher-voice, deep and smooth. He did his best to say her name sternly, but it was a weak attempt.

At first glance, he could be mistaken for a high school senior, but on second look, his broad shoulders and light stubble were hard to miss. He discreetly took her elbow and guided her to his desk.

"Since when do you call me Abilene?"

Mr. Dewar sighed. "What were you doing last night? This has to stop." His eyes were gray-blue that day, picking up the colors in his button-down shirt. When he wore green they turned the color of the ocean after it rained.

She gave him a playful pout and twisted a platinum curl around her finger. "Why didn't you join me?"

He scanned the room. A few students took their seats for homeroom. "We can't talk here. Just...stop, ok? I need you to stop."

"Stop what, Mr. Dewar?" she asked, feigning innocence.

Backpacks unzipped and chairs scratched the floor. He laughed to himself and rubbed the back of his neck. His light brown hair flopped over his eyebrow.

"Take your seat, Abilene."

Abby strolled to her desk as her best friend, Emilia Desmond, walked in. Her eyeliner was smeared, which wasn't a good sign. She and Scott probably had another fight, and Abby would have to listen to Emilia agonize over it for the rest of the day.

Emilia sat behind Abby and grabbed her shoulder. "What did Mr. Dewar say to you? Was it about The List?"

Abby turned to face her. "What list?"

"You seriously don't know?" Emilia sniffled and handed Abby a creased sheet of copy paper.

Abby rotated it right-side up:

To the Junior Class of Plainview Catholic High,
Next year, you're seniors, so you might as well try,
To redeem yourselves now for your sins and your lies.
Stop denying what you know is true.
Everyone in Plainview thinks this about you.

> *Best Butter Face: Emilia Desmond*
> *Most Likely to Get an STI: Jordan Makris*
> *Least Likely to Get a Girlfriend: Ian Williams*
> *Most Likely to Cheat on His Girlfriend: Scott Buchanan*

All the way down the page, classmates' names were listed with increasingly rude superlatives. Abby scanned the page for her name, but Abby Archer wasn't listed. Emilia's black eyes bulged, awaiting her reaction, but Abby didn't know how to feel about being left out.

Actually, yes, she did. She was offended. Not that she wanted people saying mean things about her, but anyone who was anyone was named. Hell, even Ian Williams made it. Was this an oversight or a snub? She blinked and gave Emilia a confused look.

Emilia pointed to the paper with a manicured finger. "These were in every junior's locker. You should have one, too."

"I came straight to homeroom."

Abby flipped over the paper, looking for a clue to who wrote it, but the back was blank.

She scanned again to confirm her name wasn't listed. Maybe it was better this way. What could they possibly have to say about her?

Emilia eyed her. "Well, this is, like, a big deal. Gina already showed it to Sister Bernadette."

Abby checked Gina Jaworski's title and snickered, Class Skank.

"Abby!" Emilia scolded. "This is all so mean. Why would someone actually say this stuff publicly, and who even prints things out anymore? And, I'm sorry, but how come you're not on here, but I'm basically on here *twice*?" She pointed to the "Girlfriend" in Scott's title and let out a huff.

Abby counted the names on the list. Twenty people out of one hundred in their grade, but these were the most important twenty, with a few notable exceptions, like herself.

She watched Emilia fiddle with the row of silver studs running up her ear and followed her gaze around the room. Winner of Most Likely to Get an STI, Jordan Makris, was all smiles, leaning against the window ledge, proclaiming, "I'm clean! I swear, I'm clean!"

Least Likely to Get a Girlfriend, Ian Williams, was as red as the zits on his face but laughed along with Jordan, stealing looks at Emilia. Scott Buchanan, Most Likely to Cheat on His Girlfriend, slouched at his desk, stewing over his title. Of course, he would sulk rather than console Emilia.

Abby said, "Forget about this. None of it's true."

Well, maybe some of it was true. Abby thought about Ian Williams and stifled a laugh.

Emilia took a tissue from the box on Mr. Dewar's desk and sat back down, dramatically patting under her eyes. "Who do you think wrote it?"

Before Abby could reply, Gina and another girl swarmed Emilia, each holding their own copies of The List. Emilia laid a solemn hand on each of their shoulders, like they were all now part of a chosen club. They unleashed their fury against the unknown creator of The List in harsh whispers.

Abby caught Gina looking her up and down. She mouthed, "It wasn't me," but Gina made a duck face and turned her back.

Abby rolled her eyes and turned to face front. Couldn't they see that whoever wrote this list wanted a reaction? It was better to keep the upper hand and act like it didn't bother them.

She watched Mr. Dewar record attendance on his class iPad, oblivious to the drama unfolding in front of him, and doodled "Mrs. Abby Dewar" until the bell rang for first period.

Scott rushed out of the room and Emilia hurried to catch up. Jordan held out his muscular arm in an offer to escort Abby to class, but she turned him down, and Ian seized the chance to walk with him instead. Abby rose from her chair and took her time loading her notebook into her bag. She felt Mr. Dewar watching her.

He cleared his throat and took a few steps toward her, but Gina pushed in front with a question. Abby rolled her eyes and pulled out her phone, pretending to laugh at a text. She flicked her eyes to him. He smiled at Gina as she walked away. God, she loved his smile. She re-rolled the waist of her pleated skirt and waited, but when he turned to her, his smile was gone.

She left the room for Chapel like she didn't care, feeling his gaze follow her out the door.

Emilia surprised Abby in the hall. "No wonder Scott made the varsity team freshman year. He's so freaking fast. I couldn't catch him." She gave Abby a pouty face and Abby leaned into her for support. Emilia nudged her shoulder.

"So, if it wasn't about the list, what did Mr. Dewar say to you?"

Abby smirked. "He acts like he disapproves, but I don't believe for a second that he wants me to stop."

"And we all know Abby gets what she wants," Emilia sighed.

"God helps those who help themselves," she said, impersonating Sister Bernadette's pious tone.

"Do you ever think you should be careful what you wish for?"

Never.

Co-authors **Rebecca Lang and Jennie Burke** bonded over a mutual distaste for middle school gym class and have been friends ever since. Rebecca lives in San Francisco and is a former HR manager and writer/editor for online parenting magazines. Jennie is Associate Professor of Early, Middle, and Elementary Education at Millersville University in Pennsylvania, with an upcoming picture book on Thaddeus Stevens, in collaboration with the Lancaster Historical Society. Find us at LangBurkeWrites.com.

Emilio and the Fourth of July BOOM!
by Romilda Byrd

An Autism-Inclusive Fourth of July Adventure

Dedication: For every child who shows us that the meaning of independence is celebrating all kinds of differences.

[Editor's Note: In the picture book version, words in bold are accompanied by pictograms indicating their meanings for autistic readers who have difficulty with words and communication.]

Page 1-2: Every **year**, **Emilio** and his **family celebrated** the **Fourth of July**, an important **day** in the **United States,** to honor the **country's** independence.

Page 3-4: But for **Emilio**, this **celebration** was **complicated**. **Emilio** is **autistic**, and the bright **lights** and **loud noises** could feel like a **storm** in his **head**.

Page 5-6: Every **time** they went to the **parade, Emilio cried**, covered his **ears**, and wanted to **escape** from the **crowd** and **fireworks**.

Page 7-8: But this **year**, **Mom** took a **course** that taught **her** how to **prepare Emilio** ahead of **time** so he could **enjoy** the **day**.

Page 9-10: For a whole **month, Mom** and **Emilio** became a **team**, practicing a **little** every **day**.

Page 11-12: They **read books** about **Independence Day** to understand why **people celebrate** it.

Page 13-14: **They watched videos** of **parades** and **fireworks**.

Page 15-16: One **day, Mom** and **Emilio** went shopping for **red, white**, and **blue shirts**. The whole **family** would match!

Page 17-18: **Dad, Octavio,** and **Bernardo** joined the **plan** too. **They cheered Emilio** on with **big smiles** and gentle **high-fives**.

Page 19-20: At **home, they** practiced with **parade music** and soft **firework sounds. Step by step, Emilio** began to feel **calmer**.

Page 21-22: **They** even turned **food** into a **fun game**! **Emilio** played "**try a bite**" with **popsicles, watermelon, cotton candy,** and **popcorn**.

Page 23-24: **He** discovered which **foods** were "**Yummy!**" and which were "**No, thank you**"—and that was perfectly okay.

Page 25-26: **They** chose cool **headphones** with a **bald eagle** design to **help** with the noise. **Emilio loved** them!

Page 27-28: The **night** before, **Emilio** helped **Mom** get his softest **shirt**, favorite **pants**, and comfiest **socks** ready.

Page 29-30: **Mom** made sure to **charge** his **communication device** (AAC). No tech problems on the **big day**!

Page 31-32: Finally, the **Fourth of July** arrived. **Emilio woke up smiling** and **calm**.

Page 33-34: With **Mom's** help, **he** got **dressed**, put on his **headphones**, grabbed his **communication device** and was **ready**!

Page 35-36: The **family** had also packed a "Special **Fourth of July** Kit" just for **Emilio**: extra **headphones**, **sunglasses**, a soft **blanket**, and his favorite **snacks**.

Page 37-38: At the **parade**, **Emilio** sat **comfortably** in a special **chair** they brought for him.

Page 39-40: When the **drums** started, **Emilio** felt the rhythm and **moved** his **feet**—his own **little dance**!

Page 41-42: **He smiled** wide, **eyes** shining, **enjoying** every moment.

Page 43-44: When the **flag** passed by, **Emilio** used his **communication device** to say: "Pretty **flag**."

Page 45-46: Then, with a **big smile**, he added: "**Happy**."

Page 47-48: After the **parade**, they went to the **park**, where there were **games** and **food** stands.

Page 49-50: **Emilio** tried a little bit of **watermelon** and **cotton candy**. He didn't **eat** much, but every **bite** was a **small victory**.

Page 51-52: When it was **time** for the **fireworks**, **Emilio** was ready.

Page 53-54: **He** wrapped himself in his **blanket** and **sat** next to his **family**.

Page 55-56: The **sky** lit up with bursts of **red, blue, silver,** and **gold**. **Emilio's eyes** sparkled.

Page 57-58: Using his **communication device, Emilio** pressed: "**Light**"… "**Boom!**"

Page 59-60: **Octavio hugged** him tight and **shouted**: "**You** did it, **Emilio! Happy Fourth of July!**"

Page 61-62: **Emilio**, beaming with **pride**, pressed his **communication device** to say: "Me… **champion**."

Page 63-64: As they **walked home, Mom** took his **hand** and whispered: "**Today** was special because **we** did it **together**."

Page 65-66: **Dad smiled** and said: "Every **family** finds its own way to **celebrate**."

Page 67-68: **Emilio looked** at his **family, hugged** his **blanket**, and pressed his **communication device**: "Happy."

Page 69-70: That **day, Emilio** learned something **important**: with **love, patience**, and **support**, he could **enjoy things** his own **way**.

Page 71-72: And his **family learned** something **beautiful** too: when they followed **Emilio's** rhythm, **they** were all part of the **celebration**.

Page 73-74: **Happy Fourth of July**!

Blurb: Join Emilio on a heartwarming Fourth of July adventure where bright lights, loud sounds, and big crowds become a joyful family celebration. With love, patience, and a little preparation, Emilio shows that every child can shine in their own way. *A beautiful autism-inclusive story for all families.*

Don't miss his first adventure: *Sailing Through Autism with Emilio*—an uplifting story of navigating everyday life with love, patience, and courage.

Romilda Byrd is a California-based children's book author who lives with her husband and two sons. She is passionate about inclusion, autism, and the well-being of families. She loves nature and believes in the power of storytelling to give a voice to those who are rarely heard. She calls San Francisco her golden city. Readers can find her at RomildaByrd.com.

Loss
by Selam Abraham

Every moment of my childhood, I've watched my parents talk. The way their lips form over the words they speak, the way their sentences tumble out of their mouths. They would talk and talk, and I would simply wonder what it was that they had to say. Being of Ethiopian heritage and ethnicity, I've always been surrounded by my people and culture. But I've never truly taken it seriously, because I was never taught our rich language.

People like to think that it's always me and my brother's fault as to why we can't speak our language when so many in our community here can. People my age, friends and family, will converse with the adults in their strange dialogue. They'll always be taken seriously. People like my brother and I don't have that touch with our culture. We will never be fully accepted in the community. So I try to teach myself. At first, in the summer of eighth grade, I would watch tutorials on a screen as I wrote down notes fervently. Issu means "he" and iswa means "she." My journal, once a diary full of my dreams and aspirations for the future, would suddenly be filled with pronouns and conjugations, common words and phrases. I was making progress, but extremely slowly. Eventually, the tutorials I watched didn't go much anywhere besides the basics.

Remember what I said about how my brother and I are typically blamed for not knowing our language? Well, just as long as I've watched my parents speak this foreign language, I've watched other people guilt me for not understanding it. Well, here's my perspective on this. If you teach a toddler to use a toilet, through repetition and clear practice, they'll begin to use the toilet. If you teach a child a language through letter blocks and informational and fun videos, they'll learn the language. Then how is it within my power to control whether I was taught a language as a child or not, if I wasn't even the educator? I'm sorry, but I've always been surrounded by this heavy sense of guilt, and I can't help but feel bitter. I feel bitter towards my parents, bitter towards all those aunts and uncles and first cousins once removed that have the audacity to make me feel this way, and, because of my self-hatred, I feel the most fiery resentment against all my Ethiopian friends who can speak the language fluently and are always taken seriously.

One day, as I was choosing from chip baggies off the shelf in a gas station, I began to walk over to the cashier when a woman walked up to my brother. An Ethiopian woman. Immediately, I hid behind the shelves in the gas station so the woman didn't catch me as well, and she began speaking to my brother in the foreign language. I think it was in the form of a question, but of course my brother didn't understand it. When there was a huge gap of silence, I think she realized he didn't understand and she started shaming him in Amharinya. It was pretty funny, actually, until she noticed me peeking behind the gas station shelves. When she caught notice of me, she told me to come over in a friendly voice and asked me why my brother didn't know Amharinya. I said he didn't speak it, but in a tone that suggested I could. Every time I put myself in a social situation like this with an Ethiopian stranger, it becomes extremely awkward.

Because right then and there, she asks me the same formatted question in Amharinya. And my mind goes blank as her lips form strange, alien sounds. Words uninterpretable and unfamiliar to the brain. When she realizes I can't speak it either, she proceeds to scold me in English, astonished, and asks me, "how do you expect to teach it to your children one day?" Then she tells me she was asking what my last name was. I walk away in shame. A recognizable pain. But as we leave, her question sits with me. How do you expect to teach it to your children one day?

This is where I distinctly recall having a revelation. The previous day in school, our history teacher was having a conversation with our class and we were learning about the slave trade. She was speaking about slavery and how thousands of innocent black men and women were chained and shipped on huge boats to slave away on American soil. And though this was the beginning of a terrible cycle, more importantly, it set the groundworks for a mass loss of culture. Generations of people, ripped from their roots and distanced from their country. They birthed children, and they were enslaved as well—not allowed to read and write, much less learn their own cultural language. Their children then have children, and those children have children, and whole cultures become forgotten and tucked away. I realized this was the dilemma of the immigrant. They move away from their home country, and they still have ties to their culture and traditions, but they also hold the power to continue to teach their children that part of their identity—to keep the culture running in their bloodline or allow it to be forgotten. My parents were immigrants. They didn't teach us. One could say they tried, but they didn't teach us like others were taught. I will forever be distanced from my own culture because of this. Most Ethiopians in America can speak our language and have strong ties to our culture. We still eat our cultural food, we have multiple churches that we attend under the Ethiopian Orthodox religion, and we fairly know our roots. I feel this is mainly because Ethiopia was never colonized. One of only two countries in all of Africa. Therefore, we were never enslaved by white people and shipped over and ripped from our natural landscape. We were always immersed in our surroundings. The only time anyone ever came close were the Italians, and because they had almost colonized us once, we adopted a small portion of their language, which is now just embedded in ours. For example, "Ciao" also means bye in our language. It's a loss of language. A loss of culture. Parts of speech replaced and stripped of their meaning. It's never that deep though, because Ethiopian Americans still have connections to their roots. But once each generation passes, will we continue to remember our ancestors like we do now? Will we continue to teach the language? Because though I feel bitter for not being taught our language, I still recognize our culture, but not the same way my mother or father do. I was raised in America. That makes a difference. I've come to realize that, and other people that live in America have experienced a similar loss of culture, other communities. One day, I feel like the American people will be so large, so separated from their own roots, we'll just become our own race, not just a nationality. It's strange, because everything is always in motion, generations keep coming, people migrate, cultures blend. I wonder where we'll be centuries from now. Will I be able to teach my children our language one day? Or can I just consider our language forgotten?

My history teacher is part Irish, Australian, and Italian, but it's not like she speaks any of those languages, because her grandparents never taught her parents, and so her parents could never teach her. But I guess none of them were fully immersed in their culture, because they have so many different roots. But a part of me still finds it sad. A part of me feels like it's forgetting where you come from. Because I don't want to continue this cycle that I've become aware of, but I've already become an active member of it. With so many native speakers of our language in my environment, constantly surrounding me, you'd think they'd help, but no. My parents don't really jump at the chance to, they have their own plans, their own busy lives. Even though I've so desperately wanted to learn. I'll just continue to hear these random buzz words, while trying to teach myself, but ultimately failing without a teacher and consistent lessons. I'll learn to disassociate, to become silent in a room again, even when I grow old and am surrounded by speakers having full conversations, with which I don't know if I can ever fully grasp their meaning. And who knows about the children I might have? Future generations? I can try my best, I suppose, with how much I've been given.

Selam Abraham is an afflicted stargazer who refuses to believe one might have limitations even when failure continuously snips away at her edges. Even with trial and error, she recognizes the sheer will required to carry out long-term goals. Not only does one need ambition to first activate a dream or desire, but also the determination to see it through to the precipice of reality. She idolizes those who can achieve all that and still manage to show face.

MICROFICTION

Adjudicated Winner:
Passage of Time
by Andrea McFarland

Nina, feeling odd, settled on the sofa.

Now her view of the living room arced in rapid parabolas. Was this horrifying or pleasant? It certainly grabbed her interest as an unplanned experiment. She postulated that falling would be next, as if she were six, spinning on the lawn for fun.

If she sat perfectly still, the vertigo might pass. The gas fireplace flames writhed; at the moment, she couldn't pause them any more than she could stop the awful clock ticking.

Except clocks didn't tick anymore. She realized the ticking sound came from the kitchen.

Ice cubes calved automatically from a glacial mechanism in the refrigerator. The house worked without assistance. No kindling to split, no hatchet to hone, no springs to wind.

If she fell, she would be taken care of, too. Eventually.

She gripped the armrest tightly.

As a biologist and gardener, she and life had an understanding. She turned compost piles, lifted and mixed the moist layers of carbon and nitrogen-rich waste. A robin would wait nearby, wind ruffling his brick-red breast feathers, exposing the pale down underneath. She supplied his lunch: worms and sow bugs, offered up in dark humus amid bits of straw, fallen flowers, and rotted cabbage stalks on the tines of her digging fork.

We are all compostable, she reasoned. There's an odd sort of comfort in it. No special responsibility to stand out.

My turn to be the worm.

Nina stood. The sofa wavered, an eternity below.

As she fell, her vision danced in circles again, like planets traversing the darkness.

Her eyes now peered across the bristling ocean of a blue throw rug. Beyond, a sow bug crawled across an immaculate, shining floor.

She could hear its feet.

Tick. Tick. Tick.

Andrea McFarland, raised by an English professor, two librarians, and an artist amid walls of books, has been an author and artist since age six. She's also an experienced runaway, unwed mother, wildcrafter, fiddler, accordionist, and former goatherd. Andrea may be found in rural Northern California between redwoods and the sea, along with other reclusive woodland creatures such as deer, wild turkeys, and a husband. Read more of her work at AndreaMcFarland.com

Adjudicated Winner:
At Times
by Nancy LaRonda Johnson

Standing in front of the full-length mirror, Charleen studies the accumulation of lines around her lips and eyes, etching the many years gone by. Her white afro is sparser than the days of her youth. Though stylish, her clothes are no longer saucy, vibrant, or bold.

At times, she wishes she could start over. Not from the beginning, just back far enough...

Never marrying, no thought of having kids, she'd be a traveling journalist, riding Dromedary camels in Morocco, learning to make Cacio e Pepe pasta in Rome, climbing Machu Picchu in Peru, enjoying God's creations.

Through the mirror, she watches Malcolm fumbling with his tie.

He twists the ends as if just learning to tie his shoes. "Babe, could you...?"

Charleen laughs. "After all these years!" She performs the task with attentive adoration.

He kisses her cheek. "You look beautiful."

His smile still warms her.

"We've got five minutes."

His relentless need to be early still irks but doesn't diminish how he fills her heart.

At the door, Malcolm says, "The kids hired us a car."

"Really?" She beams, sliding her arm through his.

At the hall, loved ones applaud and cheer, "Happy sixtieth anniversary!"

Their children share times of when Charleen and Malcolm impacted them most, stirring Charleen to recall: Dressing in a giraffe costume and dancing foolishly at her eldest's Halloween party; Malcolm never failing to "rabbit ear" the children in every graduation photo; the distinct scent of each of her babies... looking Malcolm in the eyes and saying, "I do."

At times, Charleen wishes she could start over. Not from the beginning, just back far enough...

Marrying the love of her life, she'd be the mother of five wonderful children, filling their home with the daily experiences she so cherishes, enjoying God's blessings all over again.

Nancy LaRonda Johnson received her first writing award in elementary school for a psychological thriller short story. A retired probation officer with a degree in sociology and a law degree, Nancy is passionate about writing stories with characters who make it through trying times and that deliver eye-opening takes on controversial topics. She has published three books, including a Christian paranormal novel which reached the finals in the San Francisco Writers Conference Indie Publishing Contest.

People's Choice Winner:
Invisible
by Andrea McFarland

My ex-husband upgraded to a girl of twenty-one. I'm thirty-six, and young men–hell, even middle-agers–look past me like I'm not there. Waiting tables in a college town diner doesn't help. I run past where they sit, lean and stubbly, with fairytale eyes and cynical mouths, sucking up the coffee and noise, no tip.

Marco the art major is my favorite. He spills his romantic woes; I give him refills. He leans near and I get a momentary thrill. It's an uncomplicated exchange. Or so I thought.

One day, he drags himself in, a melting doomsicle. He slumps over the laminated menu staring at nothing. I find it ironic; a girl a month, then it's tragedy when they break up.

"Hey, Marco. Rough day?"

His lip quivers. "I should have told her I love her." An actual tear falls.

"Oh, hey. Hey now." I touch his shoulder. He doesn't just lean, he hangs on like a cat on a screen door. My limbic system goes on red alert. Damn, I've been alone too long. I detach myself, trying to breathe. Even his manky sweat arouses me.

Later, he's waiting outside.

Oh shit.

He walks me home in the dusk, follows me in. I'm not proud. I'm fine with being a one-night rebound.

He pulls me close. His hand slides under my bra strap, his muscles tense against mine.

God, I'm exploding. I want to throw him down on the carpet. Now.

Then, he buries his head in my chest. And sobs.

"How could she have a heart attack? She was still young."

Oh shit. It's his Mom.

"I'm so sorry, hon."

"I didn't call."

"Trust me, Marco. She knew you loved her."

What now? Could I go for it anyway?

I stroke his unwashed hair. Happy Surrogate Mom's Day.

Andrea McFarland, raised by an English professor, two librarians, and an artist amid walls of books, has been an author and artist since age six. She's also an experienced runaway, unwed mother, wildcrafter, fiddler, accordionist, and former goatherd. Andrea may be found in rural Northern California between redwoods and the sea, along with other reclusive woodland creatures such as deer, wild turkeys, and a husband. Read more of her work at AndreaMcFarland.com

People's Choice Winner:
The Tip Jar
by Alina Nazareth

I rose from the rusted, folding chair and put away my tattered notebook. These were coveted seats, and I was well aware of my rank on the totem pole. Four men in suits walked up to the food truck and pulled up chairs around the shaky metal table. Not one of them looked in my direction, their expensive suits repelled by my simple T-shirt and ripped jeans. I looked at the Rolex on their wrists. I didn't need a watch because in New York, you can tell time by who is at these food trucks. These late-afternoon-lunchers were investment bankers who showed up once the market closed.

"I should've invested in NeoCrania." A blue suit sulked to his friends while falafel plates and wraps magically appeared before them, each receiving exactly what he would've ordered. They nodded to the truck-owner, both as acknowledgement and dismissal.

"If you don't learn fast, it won't be long before you are the falafel guy." Bully-bro teased his colleague. "Please kill me if I end up like him," laughed Sulky-bro. They didn't seem to care that he could hear them.

They proceeded to invent ways they would rather die than own a food truck on Wall Street. Thankfully, the conversation shifted to the shitty economy and their mortgages, and women who kept them in debt. They put the bill on their tab and ignored the tip jar. They were even in debt with their falafel guy.

"How did we do on tips?" Asked Dad as we drove home together.

"Excellent. I wasn't sure about our NeoCrania investment." I said, shifting our fully-paid-off Mercedes-Benz into top gear. "And you will never guess the tip I learned from our Brooklyn truck," I said, pulling out my notebook-log of tips from our thirty-two trucks across New York.

Alina Nazareth writes flash fiction and poetry that explores gender differences and parenting challenges through an immigrant's lens. She is a developmental psychologist and user experience researcher by day, and has published numerous academic papers in well-known peer-reviewed journals. She lives with her family in the San Francisco Bay Area.

People's Choice Winner:
Before
by Tom Joyce

Before the memorial where Kate's life and virtues were extolled in tearful hyperbole and mitigating laughter, before opiates dulled her pain and killed her appetite, before the infusions and surgeries and false hopes proffered by the next promising drug deflated her spirit, before the diagnosis she concealed from her children and friends behind a cheery charade became exposed to the obvious, before her legacy was endowed with two precious grandchildren, before her natural charm and persuasive fundraising brought professional approbation, before her second marriage to an urbane cowboy escaped its corral of contentment, before her voice earned applause and roses singing Porter and Gershwin, before the love of her life left home on his pilgrimage to the last places on earth, before closing on the Berkeley craftsman house she had always dreamed of owning with him, before that cataclysmic fire in the Oakland hills melted her inheritance but ignited her resolve, before her father dropped dead from a life too well-lived and took with him her self-confidence, before the casual affairs with married men turned messy, before truncated careers in marketing, PR and real estate derailed her ambition, before the birth of her precocious children filled her days with peanut butter and joy, before her poetic vows, flowing bridal dress and honeymoon in the Greek islands inspired dreams of happily-ever-after, before Taittinger's and an engagement ring on a giddy New Year's Eve sealed the deal, before tossing her mortarboard at university graduation, before her uncomplicated summer flings, her callow pretense to sophistication, her love for all things feline and her wide-eyed fascination with the man I hoped to someday become, before Kate, there was "Katie"—tall, golden, radiant, seductive, green eyes aglow with curiosity, passion and possibility—the grand illusion of a perfect and limitless future.

Tom Joyce is a book designer, a writer of both fiction and non-fiction, a travel photographer and a cultural explorer. His career began in the advertising industry in San Francisco, where he worked as an art director and creative director for a number of agencies. He was a partner in Johnson Joyce Brennan, Inc. and CreativeWerks.com. His writing can be seen at TomDJoyce-Writer.com, and his book design at CompanyHistoryPublishers.com

Look for the rest of these stories and more
from our contest winners and finalists as the
grow their careers through the connections they
make at the San Francisco Writers Conference.

Enter your work next time or join us
at the next class or conference.

SFWriters.org

SAN FRANCISCO
WRITERS CONFERENCE